BLOOD QUEEN

BLOOD QUEEN

The Third Book of Lharmell

RHIANNON HART

ISBN-13: 9780692406922

Author's Note

Dear readers,

Whenever I sit down to write I recall how I felt at fourteen when I read Tamora Pierce's quartets or Annette Curtis Klause's *Blood and Chocolate*. They made me excited. They made me feel like they'd written these books just for me.

But it was a memory that I'd forgotten as I'd grown up. Until I wrote *Blood Song*. When Zeraphina came stomping into my head, brazen yet uncertain, with her unbounded curiosity, the feeling fizzed up spontaneously, and I knew I had a story that I wanted to tell. I have been humbled to find that others have wanted to read it.

This series has been a part of my life for several years and I am thrilled to know that it's now out there in the world, completed. My thankfulness is twofold: that these books reminded me why I wanted to write in the first place, and that the series has found such wonderful readers.

Thank you to my family and friends for all your support and enthusiasm over the years. Thank you Sarah for the beautiful covers. Thank you, readers, for pestering me until this book was done. Thank you to Ginger (you rock). And thanks, not least, to Huw, for his patience, insight, understanding and support.

CHAPTER ONE

Islumped back against the smooth wooden bed head. A grimace, which might have been a smile in another incarnation, slid across my face.

This part was almost better than the stupor itself. The minutes when the laudanum was taking effect. My body loosening. The knowledge that, for the next several hours at least, everything was going to be fine.

A brave, brazen feeling crept over me, like I was a knight about to strike a killing blow, or a public house wench with smoky eyes and a body so tightly trussed in corsets that her breasts were pushed up around her chin. I felt powerful. Licentious.

And beyond that? Nothing. Beautiful, blessed nothing.

A key turned in the lock. Eugenia, mother's maid, came to change the water in my ewer. Eugenia was the only one Renata trusted to enter now. The woman's lips compressed into thin white lines in her wrinkled face when she saw me. My hand lifted in a fluttery wave, and I admired the ripples it left in its wake. How clever of it. How clever of me.

Eugenia emptied the basin I had not used and filled the ewer with water I did not want. Niceties for the locked-in princess. I was sure I'd read this story somewhere.

'The handsome prince kills the wicked queen at the end of the tale, you know,' I slurred, wagging my finger at her. 'Probably her maid, too.'

Eugenia glared at me, her eyes sparking with anger beneath her snowy white cap. 'Your handsome prince,' she sneered. 'If there's murder to be done it's not the queen he thinks of. He can't take you away soon enough by my thinking.'

My head rocked forward. 'What?' The word wheezed from my lips as if from blacksmith's bellows.

'With any luck you'll tear each other apart and your dear mother will be rid of both of you.' She paused and looked around, as if fearing she'd been overheard. But we were alone. She stepped towards me, placing the ewer on the night stand without looking. 'He's ugly, you know, since you spoiled his face. I've seen him –'

There was a crash, and the woman jumped, clutching at her apron. The ewer had toppled from the stand, shattering on the wooden floor.

I tutted. 'Clumsy, clumsy.' Eugenia went red, and fled the room.

Her words rolled back and forth in my mind like a ship listing on the ocean. A prince. A prince had come to take me away. My stomach hovered high in my chest like a jellyfish beating near the surface of the ocean; a pleasant, ticklish feeling. The jellyfish swam downwards, bumping against my pelvis. Tentacles flowed down my arms, making them lift and bob in rhythmic motions. I might just swim out the window. I might just swim out the door –

The door. It was closed, but I had not heard the lock grating behind Eugenia. I stared at the door handle, wondering if I could be bothered making a swim for freedom. I waited, seeing what I would do.

I did nothing. What did I want out there when I had all I needed right here? I could do my jelly-fish bob, and when Eugenia came back I could watch her grovel on the floor with a pan and broom. Nasty woman. When had she stopped liking me? I would ask her what prince she was speaking of, the one with the foul face who would murder me.

A-ha. Hmm. A tentacle reached up my neck and prodded at my brain. There was something in there. This was the problem with the stupor when it came on strong like it was doing now: things floated in the murk of my mind, just out of reach, and a jellyfish isn't much good at pursuit.

I glimpsed a face with one steely eye and one dark, mangled socket. Yes, I knew him, but who he was eluded me. *The prince*, I thought, with thumping stupidity that was evident even to me. But which prince? His face swum closer and I saw dark hair and a fleshy mouth twisted into an unpleasant smile. Oh, yes, I did know him. His name was teetering on my tongue. Then it manifested: Folsum.

I sat bolt upright in bed.

Actually, I didn't move and my eyelids merely flickered, but the sentiment was the same.

Prince Folsum was here, in Amentia? My hands reached for the edge of the mattress, out of anger or fear, I couldn't tell. The laudanum didn't let me feel much of anything. But for the first time in weeks I felt the need to get up for a reason other than acquiring little bottles of apathy.

I lurched back and forth across the room, as if crossing the deck of a ship in rough seas. The castle was pitching badly. My bare feet found purchase on the wood floor and I dove for the door handle. The currents tried to pull me back but I had a firm grasp. I turned the handle, and it opened. I fell out of my bedroom, landing hard on my knees.

There was no sign of the old biddy returning. I sloped down the corridor, palms walking me upright across the stone and tapestries as I went. My head spun. I was wasting it, my precious apathy. But a bride should greet her husband. We could pick up where we left off our tender ministrations the last time: me with a tenderised back and him with a tenderised face. We could compare scars and go for round two.

Where would Renata have put him?

I know. I'll go and ask her.

'Moth-er,' I called in a sing-song voice, wending my way towards her rooms.

Renata's living room was empty at first glance. And at second and third, too. Just to make sure I did a lap of the little room: the sofas, distinctly new and Pergamian looking (the fashion, oh, they are the fashion nowadays, Zeraphina); the marble mantle, a fire burning merrily underneath; the table. I did a double-take on the table. It was covered in large pieces of parchment. My eyes tried to focus on the scribble. Failed. Probably the sheets were gardening plans. Or designs for a moat or something equally stupid. But they didn't look like either. Lists of names and numbers. Our coat of arms. Official looking things, the sort *he* might pore over in his –

The thought was like a slap.

No. Shut-up.

The sort of thing an organised, particular person might have, someone who was making plans.

Then again it could just be a shopping list. What did I know? Or care. I was looking for Renata. There was a cup of wine standing on the table and I helped myself to it. Warmed and spiced. She couldn't be far away.

I started. Oh, there she was. At the door. Swaying – or was that me? – and her eyes gone round with surprise. Any second she'd get angry and they'd go flinty.

Yes, there it was. And now: *Zeraphina!*

'Zeraphina!'

'Zeraphina!' I echoed, flinging my arms up. Wine slopped out of the cup and splattered on the floor.

She struggled for composure, smoothing her red curls with a fluttering hand. 'Come on. I don't know how you got out and I don't *care* right now, but you're going back to bed.'

'What are these?' I pointed at the papers.

The fluttering hand was arrested on her breast. 'They're nothing, daughter.' She hurried forward and started tidying them away.

'Where's Folsum?'

Her hands stilled. 'He's here. In the castle. He never left. Now, come on.' She reached for my elbow. 'Where you're getting this stuff is beyond me,' she hissed. 'You've got to stop it,' she said, hustling me out. 'Please. Don't you think I wanted to do what you're doing, when your father died? But it wouldn't have solved anything. I know you loved him, but he's gone, and he's not coming back.' She stopped and spun me to face her, eyes searching. 'He *is* dead, isn't he, Zeraphina? Or is he … something else? Do I need to tell the guards to keep an eye out for …' She swallowed. 'No. I know you. If he were alive you'd be out there doing something stupid, trying to rescue him. Or you'd be one of them as well. So, he's dead, and that's just how it is. I'm sorry. I know you don't think so, but I am.' She marched me back at my room. 'Now,' she said, pushing my bedroom door closed behind her, 'give me the bottle. You've had your last, I swear it.'

I fell face first onto the bed and ignored her.

'Ah. There. Silly girl.' I turned my head in time to see her lift my little bottle off the dresser.

Drat.

'Send him to me, mother,' I mumbled into the sheets. 'Let Folsum see what has become of me. Then he'll leave us alone.'

'Leave you here to what, Zeraphina?' she asked passing the little bottle between her hands and squeezing it so tightly her knuckles showed white. 'I detest that man for what he did to you. But what choice do I have?'

'You can ask him to leave. Order him.'

'I meant, daughter, that I do not know what to do with you. He might.'

With a swish of skirts, she was gone. Within half an hour Eugenia was back, red-faced and cowering like she'd received a scolding from Renata. The shards of porcelain and puddles of water were silently mopped up.

As soon as the laudanum wore off I would feel very stupid and angry about everything, I was sure.

But for now – nothing. I couldn't feel anything for very long when I'd been nursing one of my little bottles. It was *wondrous*. Did people know? Did they know that you needn't feel hurt and pain being pumped around your body night and day? That there was a way out?

First it was soft. Soft as clouds moving across a too-hot sun on a summer's day. Winding around my heart like the purest wool. Once my heart had been encased, the wool seeped right into my brain and stopped the slosh of memories like gelatine setting a pudding.

And then nothing. For hours and hours. Just drifting. No sleep. No fainting. No screams or vomit or tears. I didn't have to think of him and what he'd done. That I was alone, now, without even monsters for company. The Lharmellins must be all dead now. What a curious sort of loneliness is it to know that you won't see either your most dire enemies or the one who was dearest to you ever again. Without great love or great fear I was trapped in middling grey.

CHAPTER TWO

There was someone at the foot of my bed. Or perhaps there wasn't, and I wasn't really here at all, but in the palace at Xallentaria with Leap asleep at the foot of my bed and Griffin slumbering by the windowsill. Somewhere, a short walk along the parapets, I would find him in his turret, frowning at a book. He would look up and say –

'Princess.'

Yes, but not like that. With more sarcasm, less coldness, and with a sardonic quirk of his dark brow. Then I would tell him to shut up and we'd get on with doing something interesting.

The man standing over me was dressed in a black cape pinned up to show the scarlet lining within, and a patch over one eye. It suited him. I daresay he thought so too, for it was made of tooled leather and covered the socket just so. The other eye was hard and cold. There was that same meatiness to his stature that I disliked intensely. A meatiness that might be prized by a farmer if Folsum was his best bull. Doubtless he'd be put out to stud if that was the case, but then, didn't you have to concern yourself about the animal's nature as well? You didn't want to go breeding generations of nasty beasts. If I was the farmer, it would be sausages and chops for Folsum, and I daresay I'd find another stud beast.

His eye roved over me, taking in my ribbons of dirty hair, my gaunt face. 'What a state you're in.' A lip curled.

'You're not as pretty as when we first met, either.' I was glad for my sunken eyes and unwashed night dress. Maybe now he would go away and leave me alone.

He nodded slowly. 'You never did have an ounce of shame.'

'You mistake me. I just never cared for you and what you thought.'

'It seems to me that you care for very little. That does surprise me. A broken heart and the wilful Zeraphina takes to her bed.'

'Am I not allowed to grieve?' I snapped.

'Oh, is it grief you feel? I thought it was guilt.'

'What do you mean?'

But he only smiled.

I stared at him, heart pounding rapidly. 'You know nothing about it,' I said. 'You know less than nothing.'

His mouth twitched again. 'Not so. I think perhaps I have hit on the crux of it.'

'You have not. I want you to leave.'

He came closer to the bed and placed a black gloved hand atop the bed post. 'I see you are confused, or at least are very good at pretending to be so. Let me remind you of recent events: my sister, Penritha, was on the very eve of returning my wayward bride to me when she convinced her lover to run away with her. Her lover winds up dead. Is that not what happened?'

'No. Now get out.'

His eyes went to my hands, gripping the bedcovers. 'Oh, I think you'll find that it is. That's why you're getting so angry, princess.'

For the first time since I'd returned, I missed my harming powers. How I wished I could call a bolt of lightning down from the sky and strike him through the window. But the laudanum deadened everything and I was powerless.

'There is so much that you don't know about, Folsum.' I could show him though. I could cut his arm with his own blade and drink the blood in front of his very eyes. 'You've seen what's become of me. You've gloated over me. Now you can go back to Ansengaad and find some other bride.'

'But why should I find another bride?'

'Because you would not want a sickly, ruined one such as me.'

'Your mother is a poor jailer. But she will learn. And so will you.'

He turned to go. I grabbed the ewer from the nightstand, intending to fling it at his head. But weak as I was it dropped from my fingers and rolled harmlessly around the floor, not even breaking.

Locked in again, there was nothing left to do but stew. Folsum didn't know the first thing about Rodden and me. Rodden had come to me that night. He'd been the one to decide that we were going to Lharmell. I hadn't convinced him to run away with me.

But there hadn't been much choice. If we didn't leave then, I would have been taken south to Ansengaad, flanked by Folsum's soldiers. We couldn't appeal to the king, and my sister had made it plain that she wouldn't be any help. We'd gone then because I'd needed to get away. Me. And it was to Lharmell we'd gone because … well, that had been me as well, hadn't it? I'd always been the one to agitate for going to Lharmell. I was impulsive. Obstinate. Thinking we had to do something or else we'd go backward. What was behind that impetuous insistence on momentum of mine? If it wasn't for me, Rodden wouldn't have been in Lharmell. He would have taken time to think, and realised that we were going to run straight into the crew from the Jessamine and they'd know we were working against Lharmell. Such bitter irony, that as both humans and harmings they hadn't trusted us. It illustrated so beautifully that there wasn't, nor had there ever been, a place for Rodden and I. We weren't of the human world, and we weren't of the harmings. But that didn't mean he had to end up dead.

Folsum was right. It was all my fault. That was why I needed my little bottles of oblivion.

Hours later in the dawn light I scrawled a note and wrapped it around one of my cheaper trinkets, a brooch in the shape of a tree sprinkled with a few ruby blossoms.

I tucked the package into the sleeve of my nightgown and sat gazing out the window, pretending to be pining for the world outside whenever Eugenia entered. Renata stayed away. The clouds were low and grey, smothering the Teriipsen Mountains on the horizon.

I sat and watched, hour after hour, and my mind, clearing from the laudanum, couldn't help but wander. That day came back to me again, a day not too long hence when he'd sat where I was sitting, and I had watched him from my bed with a flayed back. The sunshine had bathed him in golden light, Leap purring on his lap while he pored over alchemy books from the castle library. When I'd spoken, he'd turned to look at me, worry in his eyes.

The memory was painfully strong. How could he be so vivid in my memories, and yet gone forever?

My room overlooked a flagged pathway that led from the walled garden to the servants' entrance. When I'd last been at the castle Renata had just begun to restore the garden, which was meant to grow vegetables and other things for the kitchen, but I suspected the kitchen maids might still go there; it was the best place to gather wild berries or to snatch a few moments privacy with one of the footmen or guards.

Sometime in the late afternoon I saw who I was looking for. Geisel. She used to bring me tea in the mornings, and fresh linen. She had a sly mouth that was strange on one so young. It was she who brought me my first taste of laudanum. First since returning from Lharmell, that is. There I had been chained to a wall by Orrick of the *Jessamine* and dosed with the drug. I hadn't even cared that *he* had been beaten senseless or that we were both going to die. I wanted that not-caring again.

I'd thought that Geisel was being kind. But it wasn't kindness. She had her eye on all the pretty trinkets in my room, the coin in my purses. With practised casualness, she'd held a bottle out to me. 'Here,' she'd said. 'This'll do you up.'

I could tell from the look in her sharp grey eyes that she was pleased how eagerly I'd drank her little present.

The laudanum had been so strong that I was higher than the stars for a long time. I don't know what Renata thought, but it was a long time before she caught on. I hadn't exactly been in brilliant condition when I'd dropped out of the sky with Griffin on the back of a brant. Probably she preferred the dazed, limp Zeraphina to all the screaming and crying.

By the time she caught on I'd built up quite a supply. She locked the door, and banned Geisel from my room, but she only locked me in with my heart's desire. It wasn't an endless hoard, though, and I went through it at an alarming rate. At some point Griffin flew from my window, and rarely came back.

Then Lilith arrived, and with her, Leap. He'd been left at the palace at Xallentaria for his own safety, and forgotten by me. Leap, whom my sister detested.

'I brought him for you,' she'd said, depositing the warm, furry, comforting weight of my cat on the bed.

But I wasn't comforted, and I was too listless to care that he was there. The purring stopped, and the wet snuffling at my face. He took to sitting on the end of my bed and then a chair across the room, ears pinging back and forth, uncertainty in his green eyes. He soon went the way Griffin had: one day the door opened to let in Eugenia, and he scampered out.

Geisel emerged around the northern wall of the castle, waving over her shoulder. She turned onto the path, smiling to herself and buttoning up her blouse. Her cap was in her hand, brown hair tumbled.

I dropped my packet, timing it so it fell to earth right at her feet. She stopped, and looked up at me. I stared down at her. There was not a flicker in her grey eyes. She scooped up the packet and kept walking.

Maybe she'd just keep the brooch and let me stew in my room. But I doubted it.

I spent the afternoon tying together lengths of cords from gowns, stays, boots; whatever I could find.

It grew dark quickly, and cold. What month was it? I wasn't certain, but the leaves were scattered on the ground. Surely it was too cold for this early in the season? It felt like the air was full of icy needles, like teeth.

I pulled a fur coverlet from the bed and resumed my vigil at the window. Sometime after midnight I realised she wasn't returning.

The little harlot.

I paced the room all the next day, alternatively limping to the window and flinging myself onto my bed in frustration. How dare she? How did Geisel have the nerve to deny me? She must have all my jewels squirreled away somewhere. I could order the guards to search her room, and then she'd be dismissed for stealing.

This was the ugly side of laudanum. I'd never much liked being beholden to anybody, but right then I would have crawled backwards over hot coals for anyone who asked as long as they gave me a little bottle. Part of me was disgusted at myself, but mostly I didn't care. I didn't care about anything but the laudanum. My body started to ache and I ran a fever.

Renata entered once, and I could tell she was pleased at how ill I was. As if it meant I was getting better.

Lilith came, too. I was sitting on the chair by the window, folded into myself, arms wrapped around my body and toes bouncing on the tapestry. I couldn't stop shaking. Couldn't get warm.

She stood by the door, staying far away from me. It stayed open a crack. I could see the shadow of a guard outside. Was she too afraid to come in on her own?

'You should see yourself,' she said, shaking her head. Her eyes raked my body. 'I can see your bones. Your skin is turning yellow.'

My eyes flicked to my hands where they gripped my knees. They did look a little yellow. Especially the nails.

She stepped forward. Her voice was gentle like she was approaching a horse that might rear at any moment. 'Is he dead, Fina? Is that it? I've had a message from Amis. He hasn't been seen. Did something happen in – that place?' No Pergamian would utter the word *Lharmell*. 'You know, I'm not angry with you for sneaking away with him after I told you not too,' she said. 'I forgive you. You can confide in me, you know. It might help you to talk about it. You haven't said one word since you got here.'

In front of the entire court and Prince Folsum's sister she'd denounced me and I'd been locked up by Ansengaad soldiers. I stopped shaking and looked at her. What she saw in my face made her halt her progress across the room.

'All right,' she said, swallowing. 'I might have been in the wrong too. I should have stood up for you when Penritha accused you of hurting Prince Folsum deliberately. I'm sorry. It doesn't have to be like this, does it?'

No. I could have my laudanum and you could all leave me in peace.

'Zeraphina? Fina?'

Eventually she gave up and went away.

Finally, I saw Geisel coming, close to sunset. She sauntered, *sauntered*, down the path. Reaching into her apron pocket she pulled out a little blue bottle and waggled it at me. I threw down the knotted cords. Before tying it on she looked up at me, palm open. She wanted more.

I flew to my parcel of jewels that I'd stowed for the moment behind my dresser and pulled out a necklace, not caring which one, and tossed it down to her. She caught it neatly, examined it, and then tied the glass bottle to the cord. I hauled up my catch, taking just enough time to glare at the girl before I disappeared into the room.

The scent of soup wafting under the door forewarned me of my mother's arrival. In steamed Renata and Eugenia. A cool hand felt my brow. 'Good. You're not feverish, and your colour is better.' She studied my face. Stupidly, I looked up at her. My pupils would be little black pinpoints in the middle of my irises. Too late, I shut my eyes and turned over. With a cry, Renata flipped me over again. And she knew. I had the pleasure of seeing my mother struck dumb for one of the few instances in my life.

'Where is it?'

I shrugged from her grasp and stared at the sheets.

'You were getting better, Zeraphina!' she railed.

'Better,' I muttered.

Renata grew quiet. 'Eugenia, take the soup away. I want every inch of this room searched.'

I was propped in one corner while Renata and Eugenia hunted through every box, every pocket, every drawer and under, behind and above every piece of furniture – after, that is, they had established that I hadn't been hiding anything on my person. The indignity of being searched was nothing compared to the days aching need in my chest. I bore it quite easily.

I was careful not to look towards the window, and they did not think to go there. Why hide something in a room when you can just as easily tie it to a cord and wedge that cord between two helpful stones?

Renata's frustration grew with each passing minute. They didn't find a thing.

CHAPTER THREE

He came again. This time it was late afternoon. Or possibly early. The afternoons seemed long, grey and interminable, but I didn't welcome the change in routine his presence provided.

Propping himself on the sill close to my chair, he made sure I was watching when he clipped the key he'd used to enter the room to his belt. 'Your mother is an insufficient jailer, and I'm not a patient man.'

Reaching into his pocket he pulled out a paper twist of sweetmeats. I saw sugared violets and rosehip jellies. He began to eat them, one by one. 'Where are your little pets?' he asked through a mouthful of confectionery. 'Don't you usually surround yourself with nasty creatures? Or did you get them killed too?'

My gaze stayed steadily directed out the window. I missed my cat and eagle terribly. I'd ignored them too long. I could even remember Griffin on the journey to Amentia. It was a black blur in my mind. Snatches of forests and towns and fields from a birds-eye view.

'You know,' Folsum went on, 'your sister has turned into quite the lovely young wife. It's surprising, really.

She's pretty, if you like watery sorts of girls,' he said around a sugared violet. 'Quiet. Obedient.' He wagged the paper packet at me. 'Knows when to speak out against her idiot sister, that's for sure. Ha!' he chortled. 'If I'd but been there. Penritha told me all about it, of course. Lilith denouncing you and siding with her in front of the whole Pergamian court.' His grin grew sly. 'No wonder she skulks around avoiding you. You must have been livid. She even brought that flea-blighted moggie of yours as a peace offering and you won't see her. That's her one failing, you see: she's soft. The court, decency, everything is on her side, and still she grovels for your forgiveness. I blame your father.'

This statement was so unexpected that I turned to stare at him. He proffered the bag of sweetmeats.

'No? Well, I shall have another. What was I saying? Oh, yes. Your father. Or lack thereof. You girls lacked a firm, guiding hand in your lives. Someone to teach you right from wrong. Someone to say no to you. I wager you twisted your mother right round your little finger.'

Had he not met my mother?

'Perhaps it's not too late for you. A man could set you on the right path. A man who you couldn't manipulate. One who set boundaries and made sure you kept within them. One who made you dare not to try.' Folsum had come to the end of the sweets, and he crumpled the paper in his fist and tossed it out the window. He regarded me. 'Look at you. Silent. Not a single scowl. I like you better already, Princess.'

My mouth was dry, but I forced the words out. 'Does it bother you that I don't like you at all?'

He considered this, tongue probing at his teeth where a scrap of sweetmeat had got stuck. 'Not particularly.'

'Does it bother you that no one likes you?'

His attitude grew a shade chillier.

'You see,' I said, the rustiness working its way out of my voice, 'I am sick and defeated, it is true. I have given up. I turn from my family and Leap and Griffin are confused and unhappy with me. I could remain like this always, or I could get better.' I raised my eyes to his. 'But you will always be despicable.'

'I am –'

But he'd spoken enough words in my presence, and I continued. 'You remain here, stubbornly vowing to marry me. I understand stubbornness very well. But I have gone beyond what even the most persistent suitors would tolerate.' I looked at his eye patch.

'I will have reparation.'

'You could have had compensation months ago if you'd asked for it. Instead you send your foul sister to shed false tears and tell lies at the Pergamian court. How many other unwed young ladies of noble birth have you met at court? I knew there were dozens. I saw them myself. But none of them would have you, would they?'

He scoffed, jaw working.

'You come here and gloat over my unhappiness,' I continued, 'trying to convince yourself that you deserve to marry me. That you would even be doing me a favour. But underneath that, and not very deep down at all, you know that you aren't worthy of one even as pathetic as I have become.'

I didn't enjoy speaking as I did, but how could I even begin to think about bringing myself back to life if there was only Folsum in my future?

I could see from his face that I had shocked Folsum, if only because he had thought me too insensible to string three together. He flushed red and the single dark eye grew narrow. 'You will regret your little speech. My men and I could take this castle from your mother in the space of a single breath and throw you all out. In fact –' He straightened. 'Now there's an idea.' He nodded to himself, as if considering some point that was growing more and more favourable. 'Yes, I do think that is the best course of action.'

He strode from the room.

Chapter Four

In the morning I woke to dawn light falling through my window and striping the bed with a swathe of gold. It was a rare, sunny morning, though still very cold. The gloom of the previous weeks struck me anew. I was used to Amentia suffering through dismal, grey seasons, but things had changed, surely. The summer had been glorious according to my mother's letters all those months ago. But now the bite of winter had returned as hard as I'd ever known it.

I listened out for signs of Renata or Eugenia's approach with some fresh water or blood. No one entered. Mid-morning I heard raised voices and the thump of feet, but they were all far off, and I wondered what could be disturbing the peace. Folsum's words of the previous day, which I'd managed to convince myself were ridiculous and spoken only to unnerve me, began to unnerve me.

Around midday I heard a scream, shrill and fearful. When the sound was repeated I struggled from my bed and to my window. There was nothing to be seen outside but a glittering frost.

The castle fell silent after that. Uncomfortably silent. When shouts sounded outside my door and something began to batter it, I knew. Folsum had made good his threat and taken the castle.

I thought I'd have more notice of a siege than one bout of screaming. Soldiers battered at my door, and more out of reflex than anything else – for I had been told as a child I must hide as best I could in the event of an invasion – I hid under the bed. The door burst open and rebounded against the wall with a bang. Several sets of boots thudded in. My hiding place didn't give the soldiers a moment's pause: they overturned the bed, and rough hands were on me. They dragged me, stumbling, towards the door. Their uniforms were bloody red with black decorations. The design and cut were all too familiar. I'd seen them on the halberd-wielding guards who'd ridden into Pergamia at Princess Penritha's back, and the same shade of red lined Prince Folsum's cloaks and decorated his tunics.

I was marched down stairways and along corridors. I listened for the clash of swords, the smell of burning, the screams of the dying. But all was oddly still and silent.

When I was a child, the lessons on great sieges made up some of the more colourful hours I spent in the schoolroom. Which would prevail – the might of a castle and its fortification, or the stubborn battery by siege engines? The great battles flashed through my mind. The siege of Gorlinghurd of five-hundred years hence, in which sixty-foot tall trebuchets flung boulders at Castle Gor until the walls were so pitted they collapsed. The battle for Brid, in which the attackers used covered ladders to scale the fortifications while arrows rained down uselessly. They were noisy, long and deadly affairs. Folsum and his men, however, seemed to have managed to take the castle overnight. Of course, he'd had the advantage of starting on the inside.

We emerged into the courtyard. I don't know what I expected, but it wasn't this. Everything was strangely still. Renata and Lilith stood too one side, sandwiched between Ansengaad soldiers. They looked unhappy but unhurt. The servants were lining the stone walls. Eugenia, from within their midst, looked at me coldly.

Our own guards crowded beneath the archway, craning their necks to see. They stood side-by-side with the Ansengaad soldiers as if they were all blood brothers. None of them were armed.

In the centre of the courtyard several flagstones had been displaced and a thick stake had been buried in the ground. Geisel was tied to it, and she wore a scratchy shift torn open to reveal her thin, bony back. She was snivelling into her sleeve, one cheek blackened and swelling. Catching my eye, her face filled with pleading.

My eyes flicked to the Amentine soldiers. 'Why is this girl tied up?' Not one of them spoke. Wind whipped at my thin nightgown, and fear as well as chill made me shiver. A girl was tied to a flogging post in the courtyard and none of her countrymen were moving to help her.

Turning, I called, 'Mother, make them release her.' My voice was hoarse, teeth chattering with cold, but I made myself heard. Renata's face was raw and guarded, and she too kept silent. Her hands were in her sleeves, and I could tell by the rigid set of her shoulders that they gripped each other tightly. Lilith, next to her, looked small and pale. Her eyes were darting around, bewildered by all the foreign soldiers. She looked at me suddenly, her eyes shining with tears.

A figure moved into sight. He was dressed all in black, his leather armour gleaming mutely. A black patch covered one eye, and his single good eye bored into mine. The grey iris was flecked with black and silver. I saw hatred in his expression. If he'd been indulgently condescending up until now, he sought to make it clear that he would indulge no further.

Geisel's eyes, bloodshot with terror, darted between us.

'Princess.' Folsum's voice was pitched to be heard by the multitude in the courtyard.

'What do you mean by this?' I called. The soldiers flanking me still had a hard grip on my arms. 'This is not your castle, and nor is it your country.' Speaking so loudly caused spots to dance before my eyes.

'No, but it is my men who hold you. And it is they who will hold you from now on.'

'You have no right. This is my home.' Why did my mother not speak? She too was flanked by guards, but surely they would not dare attack her or anyone else with Lilith here. Pergamia, far more powerful than Ansengaad, would declare war if we were harmed.

But Pergamia was a long, long way away. Retribution, if it came to that, would be a long time coming.

'Your *illness*, as your mother puts it, is now over. From here you will be taken to the west tower and locked in. For a week, perhaps two. Maybe a month if that's what it takes. You will eat. You will bathe. You will regain the flesh on your bones. And then we will leave. You will not see your mother and sister again. You will not see your home again. You have proved too deceitful to be trusted. I am well within my marriage rights to insist so.'

'We are not married.'

'Do you defy my rights?'

'I do,' I spat. 'With every part of me I defy you.'

Folsum turned to one of his men. 'So be it. Whip the girl.'

A soldier came forward, a black whip in his hand. Geisel began to shriek. He lifted his arm and the whip came with it, unravelling to the icy flags.

Dozens of thin lines scored my back. I knew how it felt to be on the end of a whip. I didn't like Geisel, but I didn't want that done to her.

'Wait!'

Folsum stayed the soldier with a gesture, and looked at me, the brow above his good eye raised.

The words were hard to force over my cold lips. 'Leave her be. I will marry you.'

I'd had little occasion to visit the western tower during my childhood. It had been musty and cold as well as exceedingly dull and empty. Nothing had changed. The sconces on the walls were unused. The arrow slits were cobwebbed. Folsum and I climbed the spiral staircase alone, he two steps behind me, blocking the only escape.

At the top of the stairs Folsum paused to dig a key from his pocket to unlock the big oak door that barred the entrance to the turret room. His other hand held my upper arm in an iron grip.

The key was out of his pocket when a shrill cry sounded at the closest arrow slit. Golden feathers flashed. It was Griffin. Folsum cried out in alarm – she was coming for him, talon's first. He released my arm, and reached a large, black-gloved hand towards her, whether to push her away or grab at her, I couldn't tell. Folsum's black gloved hand seemed to dwarf her. Without thinking about anything but Griffin, I reached out and shoved him.

His hand, nearly close enough to crush Griffin's delicate body, changed course to grab at me. I pressed myself back against the door.

Eyes wide with shock, he teetered a moment, arms flailing. And then he pitched headfirst down the stairs and landed heavily on one shoulder. His head was forced at a strange angle against the stones before his momentum caused him to flip over and out of my sight around a bend. I heard the thumping passage of his body for another few seconds, and then there was silence.

I don't know how long I stood there, frozen. In my mind I saw a broken Folsum clambering up the stairs to get me, his head twisted at an obscene angle, useless arms dangling. I picked my way down the stairs, peering hard into the gloom, terrified a hand was going to reach out of the darkness and grasp my ankle.

His body was sprawled across the stairs a few turns from the bottom – he hadn't fallen all the way down. His face was bloodied, and his head lolled at a strange angle, like a marionette puppet off its strings.

Dead. Definitely dead.

I stared at him. *Now* what? It was an accident, but his men wouldn't see it that way. Turning, I dashed up a few steps, intending to lock myself into the turret room and pretend that I didn't even know that the prince had fallen.

But I stopped. That was stupid. What would I do with the key?

I could hide the body. But there was nowhere to put it, and he was too heavy for me to move by myself. I sat on the step just above Folsum's body, and shivered. My mind wasn't working properly, and it took me a long time to come to a sensible decision.

I was in a lot of trouble. I may not have been very fond of being alive just then, but I would be damned if I'd give Princess Penritha the satisfaction of executing me.

The only solution was to run away.

Without further thought, I picked myself up, stepped over the prince's body, and hastened down the staircase. The door opened directly to the passage that led to the western entrance. Dead leaves littered the corridor. I came to another spiral staircase and I ran down, circling lower and lower. The way out was barred, but I slid the bolt open and tugged at the door. I was blasted by cold wind.

I had no warm clothing. No money. No food. Not even a pair of shoes. I should have at least searched the prince's body for some coin, or taken his cloak. But it was too late for that. I stepped outside, pulling the door closed behind me.

I had not taken three steps when someone dragged a bag over my head and yanked it tight.

Chapter Five

There was a jolt. My head had cracked against something hard. I opened my eyes and could see nothing. Upness and downness were indiscernible. My extremities were numb, and by the time I worked out I was lying on my back in a moving cart, vertigo had set in and my empty stomach had begun to heave. The exertion made white spots dance in my vision. How odd, I thought distantly, that you saw black spots during the day and white spots at night.

The last thing I remembered was a bag being pulled over my body, a cloth pressed over my nose and mouth through the hessian and the scent of something chemical. What an odd way to be captured by Ansengaad soldiers, and how quickly they'd realised that I'd killed their prince.

But the more I turned the memory over in my mind, the more certain I was that there had been only one set of hands holding me; the sound of only one set of feet. And why would soldiers be so clandestine about the whole thing?

My eyes adjusted to the darkness and I saw the sides of the little cart I was lying in. My hands were tied together and lashed through an iron ring. A scratchy blanket covered me. I struggled up, my stomach threatening mutiny the whole way. Frigid air bit my face.

Ahead were the coarsely furred rump and rabbit-ears of a donkey. A figure paced beside the creature, pale hand holding the lead rope. Whoever it was wore a long cloak wrapped tightly about their body, the hood up.

'Hello,' I called in a quavering voice. White clouds formed before my face in the moonlight.

The figure paid me no heed.

'Hello? Who are you? Where are you taking me?'

But he or she ignored my questions. Were they deaf? I considered shouting some more or rocking the cart. Then I froze. They weren't deaf, they were ignoring me. It was a harming.

It was very cold with only a thin blanket covering me but I kept as still as possible. About an hour later the cart rolled to a stop. Footsteps crunched on gravel. I cringed against the bottom of the cart. A harming. It was the last thing I'd expected, but of course, it should have been the first.

The harming appeared at the rear of the vehicle, inches from where I lay.

Kill me now, or kill me later? I wondered.

It reached into its robes and I anticipated the flash of moonlight on a blade. But the hand that reappeared clutched a little bottle, a type favoured by apothecaries. The harming popped the cork and held the bottle close to my face. I recognised the sharp vapour. Laudanum. To my amazement the shadowy figure pressed the vessel to my lips and bade me drink. We continued on into the night, the vibrations of the cart receding as the tincture seeped into my brain.

Before dawn the cart stopped again and he – I thought from the size and shape of the harming's hands it must be a he – gave me blood and water. I swallowed them dutifully. Then he covered me up again, twitching the blankets until I was completely concealed. Not only was I to be kept alive and well, but I was to be hidden. How curious.

The roads we travelled were very bad. Potholes jounced and rattled the cart. I wondered whether they were roads at all, or merely tracks through the forest. Through the weave of the blanket over my face I spied thick canopies above.

Whenever I sat up he motioned me down again, glancing around like he was worried I'd been seen. I wondered of who or what he was afraid. The next day I discovered.

A mighty roar shattered the peace of the afternoon. I'd just been watching heavy grey clouds roll across the sky and wondering when my next dose of laudanum would be. I was getting more blood than I needed, and food. I'd tried to speak to the harming once or twice but he never said a word. I still didn't know what was to become of me. It felt like I was being fattened up for execution in Lharmell, but surely that didn't make any sense.

I heard the yell, and I sat up. The harming dropped the lead rope and pulled a knife from his belt, torn between making me lie down again and defending against the figure running down the hill towards us.

He was enormous, and he was travelling fast. His legs pumped within heavy leather trousers. Boots thudded on the earth, kicking up clods behind them. A horned helmet sat on his head and the cry issuing from his mouth reverberated among the bare tree trunks. Most alarming of all was the battleaxe he held above his head with both hands, the blade glinting in the winter light.

My captor grabbed for the lead rope again, trying to turn the donkey back the way we'd come. But the path was too narrow and we were trapped. The harming seemed to realise this and turned back to fight. He held his little knife up, hand shaking.

The armoured figure reached us and with one fluid motion he swung the battle axe in a vicious arc at the harming's neck. There was a wet thunk, and his head was severed. It somersaulted in the air, blood arcing, before falling with a thud to the ground. The harming's body crumpled after it a few seconds later.

Breathing heavily, the stranger lowered the head of his axe to the ground, leaned on the handle and grinned at me. Heavy, hairy brows dominated his features and his eyes were as icy blue as a frozen lake in winter. Beneath the dust and grime his long tangled hair beneath his helmet was black like coal. The skin of his face and hands was reddened and flaky.

Another harming?

He ripped up a handful of grass and began to clean his axe blade. He was filthy and he had a stench coming off him like a trash heap, but the axe, it seemed, must be spotless. With a practised eye he scrutinised the edge closely, gave it one last, loving rub and slotted it into the holster on his back.

He began to strip the harness from the donkey. The props of the cart thudded to the ground, taking me with it, until I was slumped at a forty-five degree angle. The donkey's tail swished in my face. The man pulled a knife from his belt.

I shrank back. 'N-n-now, wait –' I stammered.

He grabbed my wrists and cut the ropes that bound me. 'Out ye get,' he said, hooking his hands into my armpits and lifting me bodily out. He was very strong and my feet barely touched the ground before he was placing me on the donkey. I overbalanced, and he caught me before I fell backwards over the other side.

'Hey! Stay now,' he chided.

I gripped the donkey's stubby mane.

He peered up at me, shivering in my nightgown. 'That all ye got, girl?' he asked, nodding at my attire. Pulling the blanket from the cart he stuffed it in my arms, saying, 'Mind ye feet don't get frostbit. It'll be a bitter one by nightfall.'

Then he grasped the lead rope, and the donkey, who had not flicked an ear when its master's head had been violently separated from its body, stepped meekly forward.

'*Wait,*' I shrieked.

The stranger turned and raised a bushy brow. I pointed at the grass where the headless corpse lay. 'Th-those things. I need them.'

'Oh, aye,' he said. He bent to rummage through the bag. A flask of blood and packet of bread he stuffed in his pockets. Then he felt inside the harming's cloak and pulled out the little bottle of laudanum. He sniffed, grimaced, and dropped it on the ground, crushing it to smithereens beneath his great dirty boot.

'Oh, what did you do that for?' I wailed.

The stranger only snorted and yanked the donkey into a walk.

'That was my *medicine*, you big, stupid oaf.' My hands shook on the donkey's mane.

'Oh, aye,' he said, and I could tell from his tone that he didn't care.

Fuming, I arranged the blanket around my shoulders. 'Who are you?' I asked when we were moving again. 'Where are we going?'

He snorted. 'Hark at you and your questions. Ye're some princess or whatnot, I heard. Or ye were.' He looked me over. 'Ye don't look much like no princess.'

'Who *are* you?'

'I,' he said, a little swell of pride in his voice, 'am Raufo.'

The name didn't mean anything to me.

We began to climb up a hill. The donkey managed it easily, and so did Raufo in his heavy armour. 'Of course,' he said, barely puffing, 'ye're no just a princess, are ye?' His look over his shoulder was sly. 'You're the harming killer. I know that right enough.'

Drat.

'Ye've done this and ye've done that,' he went on, as if my activities over the last year had been mere trifles. 'But all I know is …' We reached the top of the incline and he paused to take a deep breath and look around. He threw a yellow-toothed smile at me that I didn't like at all. 'All I know is ye're wanted in Lharmell.'

That first afternoon, I discovered Raufo wasn't nearly as cautious as the first harming about keeping me hidden. Indeed, he talked at the top of his lungs as we picked our way along remote forest paths; to me, to the birds, the rabbits that hopped by. Even the empty air. He talked and he talked. Not about anything interesting. He talked about his axe, about his favourite breakfast – sausages, fried, with plenty of onions – and about his fondness for betting on the chicken races. I didn't know there was such a thing as chicken races. Apparently they wore little numbers on their backs and rarely went in straight lines.

And yet we still kept to the forest paths. When we stopped in the evening, I was deposited on another blanket and bound about my wrists again. He looped the rope around a tree.

I watched him as he laid and lit a fire, and then went about an elaborate callisthenics routine while still wearing his armour. I lost count of the number of pull-ups he did using a low-hanging tree branch. Sweat broke out on his dirty brow, no mean feat in the chilly air. Finally, he took out his axe and did a series of slashing, whirling exercises that had me wincing and ducking where I sat. One slip from him and the weapon would go flying out of his hands and lodge itself in the nearest obstacle, which might be me.

Exercise now complete, he set a little pot on the hot coals and made a thin gruel of barley, knobby pieces of carrot and a few wild mushrooms.

'I'm not hungry,' I said, when he offered me his spoon.

'It's no' a request, chit. You eat two spoons on your own, or I'll help ye.' His eyes glittered, as if he hoped I would take him up on it.

'You bully,' I said. 'Don't you at least have a clean spoon?'

'Oh aye, silly me, I've left the silverware in the bags.' He shook the pot in my face. 'Eat, girl.'

The stew was flavourless and gummy, but I swallowed a little and he left me alone after that.

Without taking off any of his armour, he lay down on his own blanket, covered himself with a cloak, and went straight to sleep.

I tested the knots that bound me. They were tight and held firm.

The forest was eerily quiet and I was cold despite the fire. I had slept rough before but never like this. It was lonely in the darkness, and as the hours passed sleeplessly I missed even my irritating captor's prattling.

There was a sound far in the distance, a rumbling like thunder that went on and on. It didn't seem to come from the sky, and there was no lightning. I listened long into the night but I didn't hear it again.

CHAPTER SIX

I awoke to the sound of rattling and saw Raufo bent over a little box. He saw me looking, slammed it shut and shoved it under a blanket.

The fire had been rebuilt and was burning brightly, little curls of smoke rising up among the bare, twiggy branches of the ash trees. We were still deep in Amentia. When we crossed into the next country, Doargin, the trees would change to oak and birch. The morning wouldn't be quite so freezing, either. But of course, at this sluggish pace it would take weeks to reach the next country. I would have gotten away from Raufo by then.

He brewed up some tea, but I felt ill and refused to drink it and he didn't press me.

Finally he stood up and tossed me the flask of blood he'd taken from the harming, now stale and gluggy.

'I'll get ye things from the village yonder. Shoes 'n such. I'll not have ye tiring this donkey out all the way to Lharmell. Ye can walk and use yer own legs. Goodness knows ye need the exercise.'

'Untie me. I need to use the privy.'

'Ye can hold it till I get back,' he said, and crunched his way across the leaf litter in the direction of the rising sun.

'I won't try to escape,' I called after him. 'Not if you bring me back some laudanum.'

He ignored me.

'I need it!' I called to his retreating back. 'I'll be very sick without it.'

Shoes. Walking. All the way to Lharmell! This was preposterous. I yanked at the knots afresh. The donkey watched my struggles, blinking long, black lashes at me.

'They stink.'

Raufo had finally untied me. I examined the clothes he'd brought from the village. Stolen, it seemed, from someone's dirty washing pile.

'Oh, aye,' he said – and I was beginning to loathe the way he added 'Oh, aye' to the beginning of nearly every statement addressed to me – 'and how long have ye been wearin' that nightie of yours? Not exactly fresh as milk, are ye?'

'Yes, but it's *my* dirty nightdress,' I said. 'Someone might have died in these trousers, from a horrible disease.'

'If it sounds like a princess and speaks like a prin-cess,' Raufo muttered as he put out the fire, 'it must be a pain in the arse.'

Without any other choice, I put the clothes on. He'd at least bought me boots that fit, and they were soft and worn in. There was a coat too, and gloves. I pulled everything on and felt warm for the first time in days.

Raufo looked me over, and tossed a cap to me. 'Stick ye hair under that cap, and leave off washing your face from now on. Ye're a coal peddler's son. We be peddlin' coal.' He thrust a thumb at the donkey, which was now shouldering great dirty, lumpy sacks. Probably stolen, too.

'Coal peddlers?' I looked askance at all his armour and weaponry. 'You don't exactly look the part.'

He shrugged. 'Then I'm a mercenary wi'out hire peddlin' coal on the side. Me wife's dead, and I got a no-good ingrate of a son to provide for. Real little bony weakling. Now shut yer trap and start walkin'.'

He made me go before him. I wasn't bound, but I knew I wouldn't get far if I made a dash for it. Twenty minutes later I was already too exhausted to think of escaping. Raufo's answer was to give me blood. Lots of it. Every time I stopped and bent double to catch my breath he was pressing a flask into my hands.

After the seventh or eighth time I stopped I was sure he'd snap at me. But he was oddly patient as if he knew I wasn't deliberately dragging my heels. And I wasn't. The physical exertion was worse than the cold. I wasn't only underweight and unfit; the laudanum had worked insidiously on my body while I wasn't paying attention. My lungs were weak. My heart raced in my chest. Spots roared up to cloud my vision every few minutes, threatening to send me crumpling to the ground. And still I would have done anything for just a taste.

Late in the afternoon I grabbed for the donkey's bridle, and missed. Raufo caught me under my arms before I hit the ground. The flask was under my nose in a moment. I shook my head.

'Enough,' I said, my voice hoarse. 'I shan't take another step.' He hauled me off the path and up onto a grassy bank and I lay there, gasping. The donkey clopped into the trees, and Raufo with it. I was alone for a moment, but too ill to do anything about it. He'd exhausted me in his attempt to 'get my strength up.' Why he should even bother when I was being taken to Lharmell to die I couldn't fathom.

Presently Raufo came back and heaved me bodily over his shoulder like I was one of the sacks of coal. A few dozen steps from the road and I was heaved off again, onto a thin pallet. A packet of bread was dropped on my lap.

'Lunch.'

I shoved it off me. 'I'll try to escape, you know.'

'Oh, aye,' Raufo said through a mouthful of food. 'Ye go ahead and do all the escapin' ye want. I'll give ye a head start.'

I glared at him, but he just grinned.

I must have fallen asleep because a booted foot was nudging me awake and the light looked different.

'We're no' going to have much daylight left soon. Can ye manage a wee more?'

Before I could answer I was pulled to my feet and my hand anchored on the donkey's withers. The flask of blood was again pressed into my hands, and I drank. The only thing that kept me from screaming at Raufo was the knowledge that if he did succeed in getting my strength up, I could escape.

We stopped while there was still an hour's dim grey light in the sky. I crumpled like unpegged washing onto the pallet. Raufo covered me with a blanket, lay another fire and unpacked the coal from the donkey. Then he went through his exercise regimen, huffing and puffing this way and that on the cold, hard ground.

There was more bread that he'd picked up in the village that morning, this loaf studded with sunflower seeds and currants, and some soft, tangy cheese, and we ate that in silence. I was almost too tired to chew. Finally, the water skin was passed between us, my wrists were bound and secured, and Raufo lay down on the other side of the fire. He put an arm over his eyes to block the last light of the sun as it cast a grey sheen across the heavens. It didn't set on cloudy days such as these, but rather drained away like water.

Bone tired, I expected to drop off to sleep at once. But my limbs ached and I shifted them restlessly. A weight sat on my chest, and the only relief came from constantly shifting about. Soon it was full dark and I was no closer to sleep.

'Will ye be still, girl!' Raufo's voice was a sudden roar in the darkness.

'I can't,' I protested. 'I hurt all over.'

'Are ye cold?'

'No.'

'Are ye hungry?'

'No. But –'

'Well ye've got naught to keep ye awake. Close yer peepholes and go to sleep.'

Rage boiled up inside me. 'And why should I do anything you say?' I yelled. 'I hurt. I don't like you. I'm your prisoner, and you're taking me to Lharmell to be killed. And I'm sorry to tell you this, but that bottle you crushed? I needed that bottle. I'm getting very sick and not being able to sleep will be the least of it.'

Raufo snorted, but when he continued his voice was softer. 'I know ye'll get sick. There's nothing to be done about it. Ye'll be sick and an even bigger pain in my arse, but that's just the way it is with the poppy-drop.'

'With the what?'

'Poppy-drop. That tincture ye've be poisoning yeself with.'

'*Treating* myself. I'm sick. You wouldn't understand.' Sad and lonely could be a sort of sick.

He snorted again. 'Oh, aye.'

'Why does it even matter to you?' I wailed. 'I'm going to die in any case. At least let me have this one comfort.' My voice cracked, and I sobbed into the pallet.

Raufo said nothing. When I opened my eyes a few minutes later he'd turned his back to me.

He awoke before I did and started a fire. I cracked an eye and watched him fry small things on a little cooking platform and flip them off into a wooden dish. He munched a few as he worked, his beard bobbing up and down as he chewed.

I felt awful. I couldn't tell what was muscle aches from exertion, and what was the need for laudanum. Raufo heard me groan and passed me the plate. I saw they were little oatcakes that he'd fried in butter. My stomach rolled.

Squeezing my eyes shut, I managed one word. 'No.'

After he'd eaten his breakfast and broken camp, Raufo held out his hand to help me up. I ignored him. So he pulled my pallet from under me, spilling me onto the damp leaves.

When the donkey was standing under the weight of the coal and Raufo had loaded himself up with his pack and battle axe, he held out his hands to me.

I glared at him.

Sighing, he reached down, yanked me up and set me on my feet.

The world danced, and I bent double to dry retch. My hair spilled out of my cap. Raufo held it on with his free hand, muttering and sighing to himself. When I was done he gave me the water skin. I rinsed my mouth and spat that onto the grass too, not trusting anything in my belly.

'Hold on to the donkey's bridle as we go along,' he suggested, going so far as to lift my hand to the harness. He led the donkey slowly back to the track, eyeing my rigid gait the whole way. 'Ye'll loosen up.'

The donkey was urged to take tiny steps and, very slowly I hobbled alongside. Every time Raufo looked at me he sighed and tutted.

I did loosen up, after about an hour, though the ache in the backs of my thighs and arms never really went away. Raufo increased the donkey's pace. Nausea hovered high in my chest and I dared not drink or eat.

Shortly before midday, when I was close to fainting, we stopped by a stream. I propped myself against a large tree root, still standing, knowing I wouldn't be able to get up again if I sat down, and I was tired of being yanked up and down by Raufo. He offered me blood, and I sipped just the tiniest bit.

'You're getting a big prize for this, aren't you?' I wheezed.

Raufo was watching a robin flit among the branches and didn't reply.

'I thought you were like me at first when you killed that harming. But you're not. You're a little puppet.'

He snorted at this.

'All right. Not so little,' I conceded. He was a large man, by girth as well as height. But it wasn't fat that bulked his chest. It was muscle. I'd felt his strength when he'd lifted me over his shoulder. He might be strong, but under all that armour, and with all that bulk, he wouldn't be fast.

I killed the last man who tried to keep me captive against my will, I thought. *I'll kill you too if I have to.* I pictured Folsum landing heavily on his head and shoulder, his neck snapping, and felt a little sick again.

Raufo stood and packed away his lunch.

'Are we to march all the way to Lharmell?' I asked.

'Aye, girl. And ye won't last long unless ye eat something,' he scolded.

'Not call a brant? It would be so much quicker,' I said, before I could stop myself. I didn't want to get there quicker. I wanted to get my strength back and escape.

'They'll be searching the skies for ye. It would be barely a day before ye were spotted.'

'Who's searching?'

'The other harmings, of course.'

I stared at him. 'I *am* some sort of prize, aren't I? What do you get for returning the traitor to Lharmell?'

But Raufo just smiled and watched the robin.

The 'flu set in. Poppy 'flu, Raufo called it. I begged for laudanum. I was weak. I was pathetic. I hated myself.

Raufo ignored every request I made for the drug. It was like he didn't even hear me. He administered water and blood. He stayed up with me all night, seeing that I did not drench the pallet and blankets with sweat, and when I did he gave me his pallet and went without both bed and sleep. I couldn't understand the point of his ministrations. I was a dead girl.

In my lucid moments I saw scratches on his hands and face, and blood under my fingernails. I woke with the memory of foul curses on my lips.

One morning before the sun was up and greenish light streaked the low-lying clouds, I emerged from a fitful doze with a name echoing through my mind. I could feel the shape of it in my mouth, sense it in the tears that had dried on my cheeks. I'd been calling Rodden's name.

Raufo didn't ask who he was, but I knew from the stares he gave me he was curious.

I was too sick to walk. Instead, Raufo shouldered some of the bags of coal and I sat atop the donkey, resting against the lumpy sacks. Sometimes I managed to doze a little during the day. If not, I would stare at the track ahead and wipe my running nose on my sleeve. I coughed. I sneezed. I sweated. I shook. I vomited up to eight times a day, depending how much blood and water Raufo forced on me. I couldn't go three steps without leaning on his arm.

He seemed to take a grim satisfaction in caring for me. When I took two small meals in a row without throwing them, he beamed at me. As if this was a good sign. As if I was making progress. I shivered and glowered at him. I might be getting a little better every day – sweating a little less, shaking a little less – but the ache for laudanum never changed. I no longer had insides of organs and viscera and bone. I had a great hollow cavity that yearned.

The skies darkened. One morning cold winds blew down from the mountains and shook the bare branches of the trees. The underside of the clouds looked low and ponderous, barely able to lift their snowy burdens over the hilly landscape. Raufo eyed the skies with trepidation. Even in my stupor I knew that this was not right. It was my own country we were in, and this wasn't the season for snow in the lowlands. But snow threatened just the same.

'Here, put these fresh 'uns on, or ye'll catch yer death.' Raufo passed me some dry, if unclean, long undergarments. The scratchy wool articles were uncomfortable, stiff and yellow with my sweat, but they were warm. We had no water to wash them in, and besides, it was near impossible to dry such things in this cold, damp weather.

Raufo occupied himself with push-ups while I changed, and when he came back he gathered up the damp garments and stowed them in his pack. Tonight he'd string them up close to the fire and fidget with them until they were dry. I'd watched this ritual for many nights, wondering why he took such care over a girl he was taking to her death.

'I'll walk a-ways this morning,' I said as he helped me up. *A-ways*, I thought with a grimace. That wasn't one of my phrases. I was beginning to talk like him.

Raufo gave a grunt of surprise. Then he shrugged. 'Suit yeself. But breakfast first,' he insisted.

I chewed and swallowed down some sweet biscuits. They were crumbly with butter and I liked their taste. Raufo eyed me with interest. 'Stay a bit, chit,' he said, and motioned me back down. The fire was red coals underneath a layer of grey ash, and he set his cooking tin on it and brewed up some black tea, adding a good shake of sugar from a pouch. When it had simmered he scooped out the leaves and added a dash of cold water. We took turns sharing the hot, sweet liquid straight from the tin.

'That'll do ye,' he said after I'd drunk a third of it. 'I'll no' have ye sick again.' He slurped the rest down and finished packing up the camp.

My legs shook as I made my own way to donkey. I'd lost what little strength I'd had before the withdrawal sickness, but I would build it up again. I had to if I wanted to escape.

It was an effort to begin walking, and I watched the steady, neat clop of the donkey's hooves on the muddy path for the first hour, unwilling to lift my head for fear of fainting. One of my arms was slung over his withers, and every now and then he'd swivel an enquiring ear towards me, or turn his head when I stumbled. His grey furry face was kind and sweet. He made me miss Leap.

I could tell it wasn't midday when Raufo called a halt, despite his insistence that it surely was, or very nearly. I slid down a tree trunk and landed hard on my bottom. Raufo held out blood and water, but I refused to let anything pass my lips. It was all I could do to breathe steadily.

While I rested, he unpacked part of the donkey's load, making room for me atop its back. I was glad. I didn't think I'd make it any further on foot. By the time I mounted it started to snow; slowly at first, a few flakes drifting down between the branches; then swirling round and round and down, settling on the cold ground.

Raufo stood studying the sky. Then he stripped his outer coat off and settled it about my shoulders. It was a strange, pitying act of kindness, and on top of the exhaustion and lingering sickness, it was too much for me. I started to weep.

'W-why are you being so –' the word wasn't kind, exactly, but it was the best one could grope for at that moment – 'k-k-kind to me?' I stuttered through my sobs. 'What is the point, when I'm to die anyway? Take them back a heap of bones. Take them back my hands or my head. Just kill me and get it over with, won't you?'

Raufo tutted, and I swore I saw the corner of his mouth quirk in a smile. 'Silly chit,' he muttered. 'Don't you know it's not to die that I take ye to Lharmell?'

I wiped the tears from my eyelashes, blinked, and looked at him. 'It's not?'

'Nay. You're to be taken for a far greater purpose than that. See how the snow falls here where no snow should?'

My skin prickled. 'What about it?'

A smile stole over his face. 'Ye've no' heard them singing at night? Nay, you've been too busy a-weepin' and a-moanin'. The tors canna even find ye in the state ye're in. You're a harming that knows not north from south right now.'

'You *are* taking me north,' I insisted.

'Oh, aye,' he said, in his quiet way.

'But if not to die, then what?'

There was pride and excitement on his face, as if he'd been waiting to be asked just that question. 'Why, Princess Zeraphina. Ye're to be queen.'

'But my mother is queen,' I protested stupidly.

'Nay, girl. Not of Amentia. Ye're to be Queen of Lharmell.'

After hearing that nugget of information, I was stunned into silence. Raufo shouldered the bags of coal, reached for the lead rope, and we began making our way along the track again. I stared at the falling snow. It was falling thicker now, and the visibility was low. I watched it land on Raufo's broad shoulders and dust the stiff, tufted mane of the donkey.

Queen of Lharmell. It had to be some sort of joke. A mistake, or a ruse. Yes, that was it. A ruse. But surely he didn't need a ruse, captive as I was. Maybe he hoped I would go willingly with him now he'd told me a crown lay at the end of my journey. But that was too ridiculous for words. Even the idea of a crown itself was preposterous. Lharmell had no castles. It had no social structure, no laws, no traditions. It was a wasteland. Zeraphina, queen of the poisoned wastes. It was ridiculous.

I sat back against the bags of coals and glared at the back of Raufo's head. He must be lying. I wasn't sure why he would, though, when he could truss me up like a chicken going to market every night. The first harming who'd captured me outside my home had kept me tied up in a little wagon and guarded me just as jealously as Raufo. But there was something about the manner in which Raufo had been caring for me that niggled at me as well. He'd been gruff, and physically tough on me. He'd needled me and ordered me about. But he'd never been brutal. At moments he'd even been kind. The times when I'd truly been unable to take another step, he'd been patient with me. Solicitous. All the nights spent in vigil by my pallet made sense if …

If I was really going to be queen.

Something Rodden had said to me months ago echoed through my mind. About how it was a great honour to bring an un-Turned harming home to Lharmell. It might be an honour multiplied if that harming was to become queen.

I shook my head, refusing to believe it. The honour would be as great if I was the traitor being brought to face punishment. The Lharmellins would never want me as their queen. I had slaughtered too many of their kind.

'You're lying,' I croaked.

'Oh, aye.' Neutral. Dismissive. He was looking among the branches for robins again.

'Why would the Lharmellins want me as their queen?' I went on. 'They have no love for me and I certainly have no love for them.'

'It's not the Lharmellins who want ye, as such.'

'Oh?'

Raufo shook his head. 'Lharmellins couldna care who is queen, as long as she is strong and wise and understands the harmings.'

'But I have killed them. I have slaughtered them and their harmings.'

Raufo shrugged. 'They are not like you and me. They be strange, uncanny creatures. Love them though I do, I'll say that.'

Uncanny. That was a word for them. I thought of their grey faces and mouths with hundreds of needle-like teeth, and the way they slithered across the ground, sometimes slow and sometimes light-ning-quick. I shuddered. They were monstrous. The habit they had of wearing cloaks, the singing, and the skeletal, pointy grins made them seem just human enough to be terribly creepy.

'The Lharmellins might not hold grudges, but harmings do,' I went on. 'I have seen them screaming for my blood. They followed me deep into the desert. They hate me. They call me the Traitor.'

'We harmings do as we are told.'

I blinked. It had slipped my mind that I was talking to a harming right then, and he didn't seem to hate me.

'I know rightly what ye did,' Raufo continued, 'and only a few weeks hence I would have killed ye myself if ye'd crossed my path. Same as any harming.' Raufo turned and gave me a sly look. 'But things have changed. And perchance ye are the best person to rule Lharmell, she what kens our weaknesses. He was very clear with his orders: Princess Zeraphina Oriana of Amentia will be our queen, and doom come upon anyone who causes her any injury. Doom come upon us all,' he muttered to himself.

My heart beat faster. 'He? Who has ordered this?'

'The harming that has asked for ye.'

'Who? Tell my quickly.'

Raufo shifted his shoulders beneath his armour. 'The king.'

'There is a *king*?'

'Oh, aye. Deep within the tors, he dwells. Beneath the earth there are great chasms and tunnels. Ye've seen only the tip of the great nation of Lharmell.'

'Nation?' I repeated. 'Don't legitimise your monstrous ways with such a word. You're all cold-blooded killers, clinging to filthy rocks,' I spat.

'Oh, aye.'

My mind raced. A king. A harming king. Could it be ...? But no. He was dead.

Then a horrid thought struck me. 'Levin Servilock,' I gasped. Rodden's old master, the one who'd Turned him in front of me, and then tried to make him kill me. There was no way I'd be queen of Lharmell alongside Levin Servilock. No amount of brainwashing or Lharmellin blood could make me forget the lifetime of pain he'd caused Rodden.

'Servilock? Aye, I ken who Servilock is. But he's not king of Lharmell. He'd like to be, but he ain't king.'

Like. Present tense. So he was alive. I recalled the glass balls of yelbar gas shattering. How Servilock had fled. He was a cunning man, and had perhaps known of a safe way out. Or down. Tunnels beneath the tors. I'd assumed they'd all been poisoned to death. I hadn't seen much as Rodden and I had escaped from Servilock, muffled in Rodden's cloak and unable to see. Others must have escaped, too.

I looked around at the freezing landscape. It was unnaturally cold, and Raufo said he could hear the Lharmellins singing every night. Rodden was dead and I was as good as. Nothing we'd done had made a shred of difference.

'I killed the Lharmellin leader right before their eyes,' I said. 'They hate me, harmings and Lharmellins alike. I poisoned a Turning with yelbar.'

'I told ye, girl. The Lharmellins don't comprehend traitors. They see no enemy but the hot south wind. Ye've maybe slaughtered them in the past, but as queen you'll put them on the path to triumph.'

He stretched his arms out and raised his face to the falling snow. 'You see this? The whole world will soon be like this. Frozen. Glittering. And you'll rule it all, chit.'

'You'll never convince me to join your side,' I swore.

He shrugged. 'We won't need to, once ye're Turned.'

That night we made camp in the snow. It fell softly atop a tarpaulin Raufo had suspended between two trees and made into a tent. He'd closed either end with leather ties and it was warm inside, if cramped. His snores were soft and rasping. Outside, the donkey stood under the thick branches of a fir, his barrel body sheltered beneath the blanket my first harming captor had concealed me with.

I went over and over what he'd said to me earlier, thoughts tumbling like scree down a mountain. Finally I couldn't bear it any longer, and with my bound hands I shook him awake.

He emerged from sleep with a roar. 'What is it, girl? Are we under attack?'

There was just enough light for me to see his face. 'The harming, the one who has sent for me. Were you in Lharmell when he gave the order?'

'Oh, aye.' He ground his thumbs into his eyes, clearing them.

Did you see him?'

'Nay, girl, no one sees him, none but a few.'

'Who is he?'

'I told ye, he's the king.'

'And what does he look like? I mean, someone must have told you at least, if you haven't seen for yourself.'

Raufo regarded me for a long moment. 'Did ye think ye might know him?'

'Tell me, please. Anything you know.' I had my fingers locked onto his filthy shirt, and he shook me off roughly.

'Get off me, chit,' he said. 'Now would ye go to sleep? I've got nothin' to say to ye.'

Startled by his vehemence, I turned away before he saw my face crease with pain. I didn't know if it was Raufo's anger or the pain of memory, but I burrowed beneath the blankets and bit down hard on my wrist to keep from crying out.

After a moment I heard Raufo lie back down and his breathing return to the slow rhythms of sleep.

It was a ridiculous hope, but it wouldn't go away: that the harming that had sent for me was Rodden. That somehow he'd survived, and this was all part of an elaborate plan to defeat the Lharmellins. Hope was a cruel, stupid thing.

Raufo was sombre the next morning. Never very chatty, he went about the business of breaking camp with downcast eyes and compressed lips.

I picked at the dirt underneath my finger-nails – there was a lot of it – and watched him go through his training routine: push-ups and squats, and a complicated sequence of moves with his battle axe. Envious of his exercise, I wondered if Raufo might give me a bow to practice with if I asked for one. Then I looked at the bindings that held my wrists. I was a prisoner. If he gave me a bow the first thing I would do was shoot him in his big stupid face.

When we were moving and I was unbound, Raufo walked beside me, the track for once wide enough to take two and a donkey abreast.

'Ye know, ye're no' what I expected,' he said after we'd been moving a little while.

I didn't want to talk, I wanted to think. 'Oh?' I said, staring off the path away from him, hoping he'd take the hint and shut up.

He didn't.

'No. I'd heard so much about this fearsome princess and her deadly companion. How they penetrated Lharmell twice, causing so much mayhem and death. The poison-tipped arrows. The wee birdie and cat that were just as fierce and slippery.'

At the mention of Leap and Griffin I felt some of last night's misery threaten to well up again. I prayed they were safe. Perhaps Lilith was looking after them. I concentrated on putting one booted foot in front of another on the frosty ground, hearing the satisfying crunch of ice underfoot.

'And look what I get instead. A wee skin-and-bone thing wi' all the light gone from her eyes and a nasty attachment to a poison of her own. All alone in the world. Where's this man o' yours, then? Did he leave ye?'

I rounded on him. 'He's dead, all right? He died in Lharmell.'

Raufo grunted. 'Aye. Well. I thought as much last night when ye woke me in a fit o' hollerin' and wailin'.'

'Then why must you pry?'

He shrugged. 'Cos ye've no talked about it, have ye? Ye've no' grieved.'

'I do nothing *but* grieve.'

'Nay. Ye may cry and wail and beat your poor bed-clothes, but ye don't grieve.'

'Don't tell me what I do! You don't know anything that has happened to me.'

'Oh, aye,' he said, and patted the donkey's withers.

My breath formed angry white puffs before my eyes. 'It's none of your business.'

'Oh, aye.' He was silent a moment. 'What about how ye were captured by that miserable string of a harming back there? Would that be any o' my business?'

'No.'

'A pathetic specimen, he was, but he must have set a right nasty trap for ye, clever girl as ye are. And you being in that big castle with all those guards protecting ye. He must have had one great big plan, that's all I can say.'

I ground my teeth, remembering. Two steps outside the castle and he'd grabbed me. He must have thought he was dreaming.

'Or did he simply wave that bitty bottle under your nose and ye swore to follow him to the ends of the earth? Aye, that sounds more like it. I can see the attraction, too. The lucky beggar must have had some peaceful days and nights wi' ye, I bet.' Pat, pat, he went on the donkey's withers. 'Oh, aye. But no' me. I get the wailin' and the thumpin', and the wakin' in the middle of the night. Is that how it'll be all the way to Lharmell, my girl? With you a cryin' and frettin' so? It's going to be a right pleasant few months, that's all I can say.'

It clearly wasn't all he could say as I could feel him winding up to a great deal more. People who say 'That's all I can say' very rarely mean it.

'This man o' yours, he must have been something special. I did hear some talk o' him, gossip like, that he was tall and fair lookin', and that he could shoot – *oof.*'

Raufo stopped talking because I'd picked up a fallen branch from the side of the track and thumped him across the head with it. His horned helmet fell off and clanged against stones. Unruly black hair fell over his face as he staggered.

A little glow of satisfaction spread through me. 'Will you *shut up*? I forbid you to talk about him.' A thought occurred to me. 'As your queen, I forbid it.'

Raufo scooped his helmet up and clamped it atop his head. Beneath all the dirt and peeling skin, his face was a brilliant, angry red. Redder than usual, that is. 'Ye're no my queen yet, princess,' he growled. 'Ye just remember that.'

I gave him a hard stare, and then dropped the branch.

We walked on in silence. I didn't want to talk about Rodden, but his assumption that I'd gone willingly with that first harming galled me.

'I killed a man,' I said finally. 'A prince. He was a suitor, and a vile person. I had to leave the castle in a hurry.'

'Why did you kill him?'

'I told you, he was vile. He deserved it.'

Raufo cocked an eye at me. 'Oh, aye. Ye don't sound all too sure about that.'

'I am,' I insisted. 'He deserved it.'

'Oh, aye. And ye family, I am guessing they were heartily behind this?'

I twisted my fingers in the donkey's bristly mane. 'Well …'

'No? And you no' but a princess? The castle must belong to someone, your mother or your father –'

'My mother.'

'But ye be in line for the throne once she passes, so I guess ye have a right to …'

I winced.

Raufo narrowed his eyes. 'But wait, isn't there an older sister? She married that golden-haired prince up a' top o' Brivora, didn't she?' He shook his head. 'I don't keep up much wi' human politics and such, but it seems to me you might a' caused a right bit a' bother for that family of yours.'

I felt a sick heaviness in my stomach, but insisted, 'I couldn't help what happened. I was trying to defend Griffin. He was a monster, all right?'

Raufo didn't seem to care who or what Griffin was. 'I don't doubt it, princess. But monsters have their own families, don't they?'

I thought of Penritha, her stony face across the high table from me. She wouldn't have taken her brother's death with equanimity. And all those Ansengaad soldiers had already been inside the castle walls ...

'Oh, dear,' I muttered.

Raufo gave a little *hmph* of satisfaction. 'Oh, aye. Fine queen ye're going to make, with your hot head and little consideration of the consequences. Well, ye can just beat us around the ears wi' branches all ye like when ye're queen, and we'll see how far it gets ye.'

'As if it would be difficult to rule a bunch of snivelling harming subjects,' I snarled. 'You would do anything I said. I could run you all off a cliff in an afternoon and then go home.'

Raufo glared. 'We might be obedient, but we're no' mindless idiots.'

'Oh, really,' I muttered.

He raised his eyes to the sky, mouthing something.

'What?'

'I was wondering what will become of us all. And yeself, too.'

I shrugged. 'I don't care.'

'No, it seems not. Ye've done a right good job of burning all your bridges, princess. Your family will not welcome you back after what ye've done – if they still be alive. Your sister will no' likely welcome ye, ye being out of favour with this prince's kingdom. It seems the only place ye have left is in Lharmell. And there's little hope for us wi' a silly, selfish chit on the throne.'

The track meandered close to a small village. Before night fell we veered off into the trees, Raufo careful, as always, to avoid crossing paths with anyone. His words had stuck in my head all afternoon, blackening my mood. I told myself I didn't care for any of it, that he'd been trying to shame me, nothing else. But he had shamed me, and without the cocoon of laudanum to protect me, I was *feeling* things.

When it came time to bind my wrists for the night, I curled the first three fingers on each hand over and tucked them against the fleshy part of my thumb. That way it seemed like he was binding me tightly but when I straightened my fingers the rope loosened. Raufo didn't notice. We lay down to sleep and I remained still until his light snores filled the small tent. Then I worked at extricating myself. It took a long time of twisting this way and that and trying to make my hands narrow in various ways, but I finally eased the bindings over my reddened knuckles, and lay there gasping. That small effort had caused me to break into a sweat.

I'd gone to bed in my clothes, even my overcoat. Outside the tent the air crackled with cold, and seemed to pull not just the air from my lungs but the moisture in my mouth and throat too. I pulled on my boots and padded carefully away over the frosty ground. Behind a large tree, I paused and listened. There was no sound. Several minutes later when I'd come out of the woods and onto the track again, an owl swooped low over my head, its wings fanning my face with cold air, and I bit back a scream.

We'd set up camp a good distance from the village. I'd planned to approach the houses and beg for shelter and protection, but the perfect stillness and near-perfect darkness unnerved me; it seemed the forest was holding its breath for something to happen. What would happen to anyone who did take me in? How would I stop Raufo just taking me back? He was armed, and these were just villagers.

And then something did happen.

A breeze stirred the trees, the skeleton twigs tapping against each other like some sort of macabre applause. What they heralded became apparent as the first sweet notes pierced the air. It was a sound I hadn't heard in so long. All those months ago, before Rodden, before I'd even left Amentia the first time for Lilith's marriage, it had been a sound that filled me with longing. Then, when I understood what it was, I'd hated it, feared it, despite the bittersweet pangs it caused in my breast.

The Lharmellins' song still filled me with longing and trepidation. If Raufo was telling the truth, would I want to rule them? I hated them, but if I was forced to Turn things I might not hate them. I wouldn't be the same person after, as Rodden had feared he wouldn't be. As he hadn't been.

Thinking was becoming too much, and with the Lharmellins' song came a plummet in temperature. Giving up my purpose, I went back to the tent and put the voices and memories behind me.

Chapter Seven

From then on, I couldn't sleep at night at all, and it made Raufo angry.

'What is it girl? Why won't you sleep?' he huffed from the far side of the campfire the next night. The snow had thawed and we were sleeping outside again. Raufo's exasperation suggested I was shunning sleep deliberately to vex him.

'What do you think it is?' I nearly shrieked. There was nothing, as far as I could see, that indicated I should not, in fact, *be* shrieking – long and hard and constantly – instead of nightly stifling my tears into a dirty blanket. The further I drew from my last draft of laudanum, the worse the ache grew for the things I had lost.

Raufo sat up and poked the fire with a stick. 'It is your man?' he asked.

'It is everything.' I rolled onto my back and stared at the stars through the stirring, barren canopy. It was late. Past midnight. Tears leaked from the corners of my eyes and trickled past my ears. The loneliness pressed down on me like a dozen pairs of hands.

'Would ye be more restful, p'raps, if ye knew I wouldn't go to sleep until you were out?'

'We didn't share a bed, you know. It's not his presence I'm missing.' A memory came to me, of Rodden drenched in the hot Pergamian summer sun, drawing a bow and squinting at the target, his black brows scrunched towards the bridge of his nose. The memory was bright with painful detail. 'Not in that sense, anyway,' I muttered. We had shared campfires as we'd travelled through Pergamia; lain side by side on the deck of the *Jessamine*, him too weak and miserable from seasickness to even speak; huddled together in the bottom of the dinghy as we drifted on the Osseran those terrifying days and nights when he wasn't conscious and I barely so. We'd been sick, sunburnt, dangerously dehydrated and blood-starved. But I'd never been afraid of the dark. Until now.

Raufo coughed, sounding embarrassed. 'Oh – ah, aye. Well, I thought ye might be feeling lonely, and I know what it is to be afeared of the small hours, like you might wink out of existence if someone's not there to watch and see you don't.'

I stared across the fire at him, sniffling, wondering how such a big, stupid lump could know how I'd been feeling. The more I fretted that I was the last person awake in the entire world, the further away sleep drew. It wasn't as if I wasn't bone tired during the day. I was exhausted. But as soon as I lay down to sleep, my fatigue evaporated.

'It might help,' I finally conceded.

'Well then,' he said, and settled his cloak around him, eyes on the dancing flames.

I turned away from the fire and tucked the blankets about me. Of course, it might not make a shred of difference, Raufo keeping silent vigil, and we might both end up tired and cranky in the morning. But for once my mind grew blessedly quiet and for the first time in a week I felt sleepy.

My body grew heavy, and I slipped into unconsciousness.

The next night Raufo tried his luck at getting more information out of me. 'What was his name, this lover of yours?'

'I told you. I don't wish to speak it, and he wasn't my lover.'

'Why?' Raufo almost taunted. 'Afeared ye might cry?'

I glared at him.

'Well go on, ye spend most of ye time a-snifflin' in any case. Are ye afraid ye might not stop?'

'No,' I said, teeth clenched. 'It's because I'm so *angry* with him.' I sat up on my pallet. I didn't want to be angry with Rodden, but I was furious. 'How could he?'

Raufo watched me across the fire waiting for me to go on. Pressing my forehead to my knees, I found that I wanted to keep on talking.

'It wasn't his decision to make, going back like that. There were a thousand things we might have done. No one had ever tried to undo a Turning before. It might have been possible, but he just gave up.' I thought of all the hundreds of books he'd pored over in his turret and the special training he'd received from Levin Servilock as a child. Maybe he thought he knew everything there was to know, but he couldn't have read *every* book. Even if he had, I might have had an idea. Seen something he hadn't. 'We could have thought of something. We were always better together. But he just gave up. Like a coward. Like a – like a –' I scrambled for the worst word I knew. 'Like a *norschuttel.*'

Raufo looked at me in surprise. 'A what?'

I flopped back on my blankets. 'Oh, just a word I picked up in the desert,' I muttered. I had no idea what it meant. Some of the younger Jarbin boys had yelled it at one another and had got their ears boxed for it. Thinking about the Jarbin made me think about the desert. I'd turned seventeen in the desert, and Rodden had given me a new bow and arrow as a present. Later that night he'd finally told me about his family. How he'd been driven to kill them by Servilock when he'd become a harming. He hadn't wanted to tell me. He'd rarely wanted to tell me anything. Why had he been so cagy with me? Had he just never trusted me?

'You know what? I think I hate him,' I said, and drew the blankets up over my head.

Raufo sighed. 'Ye're not sleepy are you?'

My voice was muffled by blankets. 'No.'

'What if I told ye a story?'

'I'm not a child. Why do I need a story?'

'We're both going to be awake for the foreseeable hours, it seems,' he said, and I didn't miss the accusation in his voice.

It's your fault for asking me his name, you stupid oaf, I fumed. 'Whatever you like,' I said, and rolled away from him.

'This is a story from the desert,' he began.

It was on the tip of my tongue to tell him I didn't want to hear about the desert, that I knew all about the desert, thank you, and that if he didn't shut-up about the stupid desert I was going to have a screaming fit right there on the ground. But I closed my mouth again. I didn't know the desert stories, after all, whereas I'd heard most of the Brivoran tales. I closed my eyes, but my ears stayed open.

He began.

'There was once a king called Hirym who loved his wife so much that his heart near beat out of his chest at the sight o' her. His younger brother, also a king, called Gramash, loved his wife also, and the two men were happy.'

Raufo spoke softly and slowly, and I felt my body relaxing.

'The brothers ruled neighbouring kingdoms, but so very far apart the palaces were that twenty years went by without one setting eyes on the other. So Hirym sent the vizier, his minister, across the desert with a letter for Gramash, entreating him to come.

Gramash missed his brother too, and immediately set about making plans to cross the desert with his retinue. Not many days later, he departed with his horses and tents and men, and he bid a sweet adieu to his wife.

'That first night when they made camp, King Gramash remembered he had left a very important gift behind, something he particularly wanted to give to his brother. So he took one of his fastest horses and galloped all the way back to the palace.

'Upon entering his bedchamber he came upon his wife, lying naked on the carpets. She was with one of the kitchen slaves, a brute of a man, foul with grease and dirt.

'Crying out, Gramash drew his sword and, with one stroke, cut their heads from their bodies where they lay.

'Saying nothing of what he had seen or what he had done, he left the palace and returned to his men, and continued the trek across the desert. But his heart pained him. He grew weak and sallow, refusing food and retreating into a caravan. By the time he reached his brother's palace he was very sick, but he still kept the secret of his wife's infidelity. To his brother, who was concerned to see him so altered, he said, "Do not fear, it is the journey that has lowered my spirits. I shall be much better once I have rested."

'But he wasn't better. He languished in his brother's palace for weeks, unable to take pleasure in anything: the grounds, the cool air, or even his beloved brother's company.

'Hirym proposed many diversions, but Gramash refused them all. On the day Hirym intended to hunt, Gramash's reply was the same: "Dear brother, I would, but I have not quite got my strength back. You go, and I will join you as soon as I am better."

'Hirym went, and Gramash walked aimlessly through the palace. He soon found himself in the pleasure gardens, and, sitting behind a screen, hoped to find some peace in which to think upon his wife and her betrayal. His solitude was interrupted, however, by the entrance of nine female slaves, and nine male. They were naked, and lay on the soft grass, and began to set upon one another with passion. Moments later, Hirym's wife appeared in their midst. She was a comely woman, and, Gramash had thought, a model of virtue and modesty. Doffing her clothes she cried out, 'Come to me, my lover!' and from out of a tree slid a man with a snarling, lustful face. He grabbed Hirym's wife, and Gramash watched as they joined the twining bodies around them.

'Later, Gramash thought hard and long about what he had seen, and found his spirits strangely lightened. If Hirym's wife was just as unfaithful as his own, and with an equally lowly, wretched specimen, did this not mean that the fault of the infidelity lay with women, all women, rather than due to any shortcoming of his own or his brother's? For who but a polluted person would choose to lay with such men?

'When Hirym returned from the hunt he found his brother well rested and well fed; better, in fact, that he'd seemed during his whole visit.

"What has caused this wondrous transformation?" Hirym asked. Gramash replied, "Nothing that needs speaking of, my dear brother." But Hirym insisted, despite Gramash's protests that it would bring him no pleasure to hear.

'Finally, Gramash said he would show Hirym what had caused his transformation, but they would have to organise another hunt. The very next day they did, and when they'd ridden out of sight of the palace with their men they made camp, and the pair turned back. At the palace, Gramash showed him the screen in the pleasure garden that had secreted him, and there they lay in wait. Soon entered the nine slave women and the nine slave men, who stripped and lay down together. Then came Hirym's wife, who called to her lover in the tree.

'Gramash bade his brother depart then, but Hirym insisted on staying to witness his wife's infidelity. When it was over they left, and Hirym called his vizier to him. With passion he cried, 'Take my wife to the executioner at once. I wish to never look upon her again. Then fetch me a virgin and I will marry her tonight. Come morning, she will be executed too. I will take another wife tomorrow night, and every night thenceforth, and they shall all die upon the sunrise. For women are deceitful creatures worthy of no more than a swift death. None shall betray me again."

'The vizier did as he was told: the king's wife was executed and a new bride found. As soon as the dawn light touched the palace, she was taken to her death. King Hirym married another that evening and she too was dispatched when morning came. This continued for two years, whereupon there was public outcry from the parents over all the daughters who had died, and from the young men who had no one to marry.

'The vizier mentioned to his king the difficulty he was having finding young women for him to marry. "Do you not have two daughters of your own?" the king asked.

'With a heavy heart the vizier returned home. He did indeed have two daughters, both beautiful and intelligent. The younger, Jaseen, was particularly well-read and witty, and when she'd heard her father's sad duty, she insisted on being offered to the king before her elder sister. "For I have a plan, and if I fail I shall have fared no worse than had I let my sister go first; but if I succeed I will save her and myself, and all the other women who would have followed."

'The vizier agreed, and that night she was married to King Hirym. As the pair lay upon the carpets in his bedchamber, Jaseen began to tell the king a story.'

I waited for Raufo to continue, but his silence stretched into the darkness. 'What was the story she told him?' I muttered into the blankets.

'Hush now,' he whispered. 'Ye're tired. I'll tell ye the rest of the story tomorrow.'

'Did he kill her in the morning?'

But Raufo was pulling his blankets around him. 'Don't fret yeself. I'll still stay awake till ye are asleep.'

Almost despite myself, I slept.

The morning was a clear one, and the sun reflected brightly off the frost-laced branches. The trail we followed was barely visible but for the depression it made in the ground. As we made our way through the trees I spied the paw-prints of foxes and other small creatures who'd been abroad far earlier than we. How were they faring in this long winter? And the birds? Not a leaf or blossom could be seen on the trees; not even a nub of one that would herald the spring.

I did not realise I'd even been thinking of the story until I blurted, 'Raufo, I do not like Gramash.'

From the other side of the donkey, Raufo raised his eyebrows at me. 'Oh, aye. And why would that be?'

I frowned. 'For several reasons. His health improved when he discovered his brother's wife was an adulterer just like his own, first of all.'

'Aye. And why should it not?'

'Well, it's just ridiculous! The infidelity should make him sad for his brother, not bring his appetite back. And I don't believe for a second that he truly wished to keep his brother ignorant of his wife's lover. When you say to someone, "Oh, I feel better, but I cannot tell you the reason," it is meant to deliberately inflame the other's curiosity. If he'd said nothing but that he felt better for no reason, Hirym would never have pressed him on the matter.'

'Perhaps so.'

'No, absolutely so. He wanted his brother to know.'

'And d'ye not agree that a person should know when their wife be a-carrying on behind their back?'

I frowned. 'I don't know. It is the underhanded way Gramash went about it that I don't like.'

'It is interesting ye find the most fault with Gramash, when he only murdered two, in a fit of passion, and Hirym executes hundreds in cold blood.'

We walked on silently for a while, but my mind was not restful. 'Why did the queens choose such despicable creatures for lovers?' I asked. 'You said they were brutes, foul and unwashed. It makes little sense that a queen would choose to take such a person to their bed. Are there no handsome, clean men among the slaves? Could she not entice a guard with a fine figure and a habit of bathing?'

'Perhaps she wished to abase herself as an insult to her husband.' Raufo was amused by all my questions.

'That makes no sense. The infidelities were conducted in secret. How were the queens supposed to insult their husbands if they never found out? Unless they knew how risky it was and wanted them to find out.'

Raufo nodded. 'Aye, I'd say they knew the risks all right.'

'It sounds to me like the storyteller is siding with Gramash and Hirym: all women are polluted and worthy of death, even the virgins who can't be trusted with even one day's wedded life.'

'I only tell ye the stories as I heard them,' Raufo said.

'Yes, well. I am sure the storyteller you heard it from was a man, and all were men right back to the first telling.'

He let out a roar of laughter. 'I can tell this princess has been brought up in Amentia, and that's for sure.'

'What do you mean?'

'A-harkin' to the train of your thoughts: all innocence be the women and all guilty be the men. It is as if ye were raised in a queendom,' he mocked.

'Rot. I just know more about the men in this case than I do the women. Murder is worse than adultery.'

He chuckled. 'Oh, aye.'

We were silent for several minutes, but the smile didn't leave his face; I kept sneaking looks at him across the donkey's withers.

'What?' I finally asked. 'What has you so amused?'

His grin only broadened. 'Nothing at all, chit.'

'Will you tell me the rest of the story now?'

'Nay, that story is for bedtime. We have a long day ahead of us before then.'

Once I was settled on my pallet that night, he resumed the story.

'This is the tale that Jaseen told the king.

'In a land far away, a land of gods and war, lived a girl called Pollixia. Pollixia was the youngest of eleven, with ten older brothers, and the daughter of a great warlord. One day there came a visitor to the villa, a huge man in battle leathers and a great black cloak. He sat in conference with Pollixia's father while all the family waited outside, straining to hear. For this was no ordinary man. He was the supreme god, Tanah. A battle god, as fearsome as they come. He was present at every battle, and his handmaidens rode white horses over the battle-field, deciding who would fall and whose sword would strike true.

'Finally Pollixia was called into the room, along with her brothers and mother. Tanah sat at the head of the table, silent and fearsome. Pollixia was afraid, because Tanah's visit could only mean war, and her father and brothers might die.

'"Pollixia," said her father, "a great honour is to be bestowed on you. You are to become one of Tanah's handmaidens."

'All her brothers suddenly crowded round her, touching her braids and kissing her cheeks. Pollixia knew that they were happy because having her as a handmaiden to Tanah meant that they would not fall in battle with her to look out for them.

'Pollixia bowed to her father and bid goodbye to her mother and brothers, for she knew she would be leaving with Tanah that very hour.

'In the Great Halls of the gods, high above the land, Pollixia learned that there was to be a battle, and that her father and brothers would all be fighting. She readied herself with the other handmaidens, donning light, golden armour and white robes, and saddling her white horse.

'Before the battle, Tanah sent for her. She knelt before the god, ready to receive her orders as to who would fall and who would live. It didn't matter to her who must fall, as she would be able to keep her father and her brothers safe.

'Tanah spoke. "You must see to it that your father and all your brothers die in this battle."

'"But my lord!" gasped Pollixia. "Why must I do this? They are good men and serve you devotedly."

'"They do. But they must all die on the morrow."

'They are all expecting me to keep them safe. Please, tell me why this must be so."

"Your grandfather did not honour me. His brothers did not honour me. Your family must pay for this insult."

"*We* honour you," Pollixia insisted. "My family have always honoured you, and serve your purpose."'

Raufo stopped. With an effort, I cracked an eye open. 'What did she do?'

'That's a story for tomorrow,' he said softly.

'But what did Jaseen do when the morning came?' I asked, not forgetting about the king Hirym and his young wife. 'I'm not tired yet,' I lied.

'Oh, aye. Go to sleep, chit.'

Eyes heavy from the slow cadence of his voice, I went to sleep.

The following day was much like the others that preceded it. Cold, wearying, and dull. But I had the tales of Jaseen and Pollixia in my head. Jaseen the clever and Pollixia the obedient. But how obedient was Pollixia? I felt sure that she wasn't going to murder her own family, and instead that she'd turn out to be just as clever as Jaseen and figure out a way to save them all. I wondered all this aloud, hoping to draw some nuggets of the tale from Raufo, but he only smiled his secretive smile.

In the middle of the afternoon I heard the distant roaring sound that I'd heard once before. I paused, and so did the donkey. 'Did you feel that?' I asked Raufo.

He frowned, looking around him as if he was trying to discern its origin. 'Aye. I heard it too.'

'What is it?'

'I dinna ken.'

'I have heard it before, late at night.'

'So have I. It is like thunder, but it seems to come up from the earth, not down from the sky.' We waited a few moments but the sound didn't come again. After a while Raufo clicked his tongue at the donkey and we moved on.

Night fell, and I lay on my pallet bundled in blankets. 'Tell me what happened to Pollixia,' I demanded.

Raufo sat before the fire, poking it with a green stick that sizzled with sap. 'Close your eyes,' he said.

'Go on, then,' I said, eyelids closed.

'Well, Jaseen stopped the tale just where I stopped it, and the king asked her a hundred questions about Pollixia and the god and her family. But she wouldn't tell him anything. Eventually they both went to sleep, and upon the morning, the king couldn't bring himself to execute her without hearing the rest of the story. Jaseen promised to continue the tale that night, so Hirym granted her another day, but told himself he would execute her as soon as the morning came.

'Jaseen told the king that Pollixia, bereft by Tanah's orders, threw herself from the Great Halls in the sky and her body was dashed upon the ground, and she died. Another handmaiden was given Tanah's instructions, and Pollixia's father and all her brothers died in battle.'

My eyes snapped open. 'What!'

'I said –'

'I heard what you said. But the story can't end that way.'

'Why not?'

'Because that's a *terrible* ending.'

Raufo shrugged. 'An ending's an ending.'

I sat up to object, but he put a hand out. 'Lie down, chit. These stories are meant to help ye sleep. Do ye no want to hear about Jaseen?'

Yes, there was still Jaseen. She was much cleverer than poor Pollixia, who couldn't save a single member of her family, or even herself.

'Now, close y' eyes again and I'll go on. They're closed? A'right then. So, as soon as Jaseen finished her tale of Pollixia and the god Tanah, she began another.

'In a place far from where Pollixia lived, and in a very different time, lived a young husband called Dyso. Dyso was a good man and an obedient son, but deep down inside he nursed the fear that he might one day kill whom he most loves. Dyso kept this fear at the darkest corners of his mind, for everyone has fears and most of them are quite irrational. He reasons that, after all, it must be a very simple thing to refrain from killing who he most loves – a person is much more likely to kill that who he most hates, surely. But still, he had nightmares every now and then, and the worst one yet was on his wedding night.

'Dyso had just married a very pretty daughter of an important man in the next village and she had come to live with him and his mother and father. This was the way of his people, that when a young married man of slim means takes a wife she comes to live with his family until he has saved enough to set up his own little house.

'His bride, Petuna, was respectful to his father and made herself useful to his mother. Dyso was happy.

'One cold winter's night, not many weeks after Petuna had come to live with them, the family was sitting around the fireplace in contented silence. A good meal was in their bellies and they felt warm and comfortable, all the more for hearing a thunderstorm beating on the shutters of their secure little home, and the wind whistling under the eaves. Dyso had a fat tabby cat on his lap, shedding and purring with closed-eyed bliss as he scratched the cat's cheek. He watched his bride from across the room, and felt content.

'Petuna was sitting quietly, her hands folded in her lap, eyes tracing the edges of the shutters where lightning would show as it flashed. There was a loud crack of thunder and a shadow passed across Petuna's face.

'"What is it, my love?" Dyso asked quietly.

'She turned to him with a shudder. "I don't like lightning. I am afraid of it."

'"Tis just a storm. It will pass."

'"I know, but I am afraid anyway," she said with a little laugh. "What are you afraid of?"

'Dyso was silent. He knew what he was afraid of, but he didn't want to talk of it. When he didn't answer, Petuna looked to his mother and father for their answers.

'His mother glanced with distaste at the cat on Dyso's lap. She didn't like animals in the house, thinking they were dirty creatures that carried disease. There was disease everywhere, after all, so what was to be gained by inviting it into your nice clean home? But the cat kept down the mice which were wont to spoil the flour, and filthy mice in the flour was far worse than one tabby cat. "Sickness," she muttered. "Sickness in my house that I can't keep out. Which I might carry here."

'Dyso's father listened to the wind howl, and worried about the cows in the byre. What if he'd not built it strong enough, and it collapsed and killed the beasts? Easily enough the words slipped out: "That through my folly or carelessness I won't provide for you all."

'Petuna listened to them, and then she said, "My true fear is that I will be a shrewish and demanding wife, and that Dyso won't love me anymore."

'Dyso remembered the nightmare he'd had on his wedding night. That he'd taken his bride down to the river and waded out with her, took her in his arms and held her under the water till she was dead. "Eels," he lied. "I can't abide the sliminess of eels."

'Petuna started to protest that eels wasn't a real fear, when Dyso's father stood up and pronounced that it was late and they should all go to bed.

'The weeks passed, and Dyso's pretty bride settled into the day-to-day life of the small holding. It was much smaller than what she'd been used to, but she loved Dyso and told herself that it didn't matter. She had nice gowns, but didn't have the chance to wear them tending the vegetable garden. She liked to arrange things just so, but couldn't when Dyso's mother only arranged them back to the way they were. Her hands had been soft and her nails pink, but now her skin was scored with dirt or flaked from washing up dishes and laundry.

'Things would be much better, she told herself, when she and Dyso had their own little house. But when she asked her husband when they would be able to afford it, he said it would take quite some time. Years, in all probability.

'Petuna was vastly disappointed, but because she was determined not to be a shrewish wife and she kept her dissatisfaction to herself. Inwardly, though, she made a plan.

'Taking a little of her housekeeping allowance, Petuna stole away in secret. She was gone for many hours and as it began to grow dark, Dyso became worried. Finally she returned, flushed and trembling, but smiling. At his many questions, she laughed and said she'd been to visit her family on a whim, and had anything of consequence happened while she'd been gone?

'Just then there was a knock at the door, and Dyso opened it to find one of the wealthy landowners of the village standing on the doorstep. This man could boast many hectares of grazing land rather than the little plot of barley that Dyso's family worked. But they had one other plot of land, this one in Dyso's name. It was a little ways out of the village, and too marshy for barley, but he often took the goat there to graze its fill. It was this plot that the farmer had come about. He needed to expand onto Dyso's land, and could he buy it? The man offered a huge sum for it, and Dyso was quite taken aback.

'Before he could say anything, Petuna hastened forward and agreed that of course they would sell it, and the thing was done.

'After the farmer had left Dyso stood looking at the coins in his hand. It was more money than he'd ever seen in his life. Something troubled him about the sale, and he said to Petuna, "It is very strange to offer so great an amount of money for such a poor piece of land. And I do not think it right that you should agree to sell my land for me."

'Petuna's face grew dark and her eyes small, and she stated that only a fool would not take advantage of such an offer. Dyso was taken aback by her manner, but he was silent, and went uneasily to his bed.

'Petuna wasn't quite herself after the sale. All she could talk about was the money they now had and how she wanted him to use it for this and then that. He grew quite sick of her talking about it and, mulish, refused to do anything with the money at all. Petuna stopped speaking to him and spent all her time with his mother instead.

'One day the two women were absent a long time together, and when they finally returned they wore secretive smiles and giggled to one another. But all they said was that they had been to the market. A travelling salesman had been in the town and they'd bought some old tin plates and trousers. Dyso's mother gave him the trousers, and though he didn't want them as they were worn and a little dirty, Petuna seemed as if she was going to burst into angry tears if he objected, he put them on.

'The next morning Dyso woke to find boils had broken out all along his legs and he felt weak and feverish. Petuna bade him stay in bed and brought him cooling tea. He slept fitfully, and when he woke he felt worse. There were swellings at his groins and armpits.

'A very expensive doctor was brought in to treat him, and Dyso was bled with leeches and given drafts to drink. After, his mother sat with him, silent tears ran down her cheeks.

'"What is it?" he asked

'"I have done this," she replied. "It was those trousers I bought for you, I am certain. The salesman insisted I take them with the plates, though I protested I didn't want them. They must have been filled with sickness." And she took the trousers from where they lay over a chair and thrust them into the fire.

'Dyso protested that it was surely something else, for who had heard of trousers making anyone ill?

'The next day Petuna rushed into the bedroom where Dyso lay, as happy as she could be, exclaiming that the old tin plates they'd bought were really gold, and she'd sold them for an extraordinary sum of coin. He had to get up so they could choose their own house to live in. Dyso protested that he couldn't get up –he was too sick. Petuna stamped her feet and raised her voice, and shouted that they were never going to leave and that he was always finding excuses. Dyso was more worried than ever about his wife's behaviour, but was unable to follow her when she ran out of the room.

'He grew no worse over the following days, but he also grew no better. Petuna stayed away from him. One morning his mother brought up a letter to him addressed to his father, and together they wondered whom it could be from, as letters were rare things in their little house. "Call my father and he shall open it," said Dyso.

'"I can't, he is out with Petuna."

'For some reason worry flashed through Dyso at her words, but he didn't know why.

'At dusk he heard screams, and Petuna came running up the stairs in a great fright. "Oh, Dyso, Dyso, come quickly! Your father is slaughtering the cows!"

Dyso struggled out of bed and down the stairs to find his mother sobbing in the kitchen. He went out to the byre to find their three cows dead in their stable and a great deal of blood on the ground. His father was standing silently, still gripping the knife.

'"Father, why have you done this?" Dyso cried.

'"I thought the cows had caught the sickness. There was a boil on one of their noses and you must kill your cattle if you find a boil, lest all the cows in the village catch the sickness."

'Dyso checked the cows. "There are no boils on any of them."

'All his father could repeat was, "I thought there was."

'Back inside his mother was still sobbing, and Petuna was holding the letter that had arrived in the morning. "You needn't worry, Dyso,' she said with a smile. 'A relative has died, and he's left your father some money."

'Dyso was feeling very ill and he took himself to bed, unable to answer. He was certain that there was something gravely afoot in the household. He remembered the conversation they'd had the night of the storm when they'd shared their worst fears: Petuna's worry she would become shrewish; his mother's fear of bringing disease into the house; his father that he would destroy their livelihood.

'Going to his mother, he questioned her about Petuna and if she'd done anything strange of late. Reluctantly, his mother finally said, "I will tell you."'

Raufo stopped there, and as sleepy as I was I said, 'Well? What did she say?' But Raufo only grunted and said that that was quite enough for one night, and that there was no point going on as I'd only fall asleep before he got to the end.

'Rot,' I muttered. But after a few minutes I fell asleep.

In the morning Raufo was a ways away and hunched over his little wooden box with his back to me. There was the usual furtiveness to his shoulders.

Well, *let* him be furtive. What did I care what was in his silly box?

'Take care I don't see what's inside, I'm awake now,' I called.

Raufo half-turned and glared at me. 'An' so ye should be, lazybones,' he said, as if he didn't care what I might see. But he slammed the box shut.

After he'd unbound my wrists so I could stoke up the fire, Raufo ran through his gamut of exercises: lunging steps and body presses and hauling his chin up to reach a tree branch using only his arms. He grunted and sweated and went very red in the face.

Feeling restless, I hunted through the food pack and found the skillet, and began frying some old heels of bread in butter, before cracking two eggs over them.

With an interested quirk of an eyebrow, Raufo finished his routine and wandered over. 'What do you call this, then?' looking at the crispy hunks of bread and fried egg.

Shrugging, I said, 'Breakfast. But I doubt it's very good.'

'Tis always sweeter when it's someone else has cooked it,' he said appreciatively, and sat down to devour his portion with more than a little relish. It was an unusually bright day, and I felt better than I had in a long time. The packs weren't like lead weights in my arms and I was able to help lift them onto the donkey. When we set off, I didn't get breathless until the path began to incline slightly. The cold wind was freshening on my cheeks instead of numbing. I was burning with curiosity about Dyso and Petuna, and Jaseen too, but didn't bother to ask Raufo about them. I knew he wouldn't tell me anything until tonight.

When we made camp I was so anxious for him to continue the tale that I cooked the evening meal as well, boiling up some cracked grains with a ham hock and some dried peas into a thin stew. I'd added too much salt to the already salty hock, and it was quite flavourless otherwise, but Raufo was quite appreciative despite this.

'Where did ye learn to cook?' he asked, scraping up the very last of the meal and swallowing it down with a satisfied sigh.

'I didn't. I've been watching you.'

Finally we were both settled on to our pallets and he continued the tale. Raufo cleared his throat and stirred the fire. 'So, we were with Dyso and his mother, and he was asking her if anything strange had happened of late.

'Dyso's mother told him that Petuna had taken her not just to the market the day they'd bought the diseased trousers and gold plates, but also to a friend on the outskirts of the village. This friend was a woman called Wurgrot, and she gave Dyso's mother a bad feeling. But if this was a friend of Petuna's she wasn't going to be rude.

'Dyso's mother said, "Petuna began to talk, as she does these days, of how much better our lives would be if we were all prosperous and she and you could move out of our cramped little house and into your own. And she pressed me to say the same. It wasn't enough for me to agree with her politely. I had to say it myself. And she is so very *pushy* these days. Immediately I had said it I wanted to take the words back, for there was such a cunning look in this strange woman's eyes and I didn't like it at all."

'Dyso went to his father and he told much the same story, and also where he could find this woman. He'd never heard Petuna talk of any friend by the name of Wurgrot. Without telling Petuna, and as unwell as he was, Dyso went to find her.

'At Wurgrot's house the woman who opened the door was unknown to him. But she bade him come in and made him tea. The woman was just so ordinary that Dyso began to think his mother and father had greatly exaggerated their unease. But the woman pressed him to talk about his wife and his family, and before he knew what he was about he'd said that his life might be a lot better if he and Petuna had the means to live alone.

'Immediately he'd spoken the words Wurgrot took away his tea and bade him go because she was busy.

'On the walk back to the village he came across a gentleman leading a very fine horse. The lord hailed him and led the horse over to Dyso. It was a beautiful grey gelding with liquid brown eyes and a soft mane and tail. He'd never seen so fine and gently bred a horse in his life.

'"Friend, I am journeying over the sea to meet my bride and it is unlikely I shall return for many years. There is no one to take my horse, so I would give it to you."

'Dyso protested that surely he should sell it at the market as it would fetch a very fine price.

'"There is no time,' said the noble. "The carriage taking me to my ship is in the village and I must go now, and there is no one to look after my horse.'

'Dyso had always wanted a horse such as this one, and the noble did entreat him so. He took the reins from the man and he rushed off, calling "A thousand thanks!"

'As he stroked the horse's velvety nose, a queer feeling came over Dyso. An angry feeling. He was ill at his mother's hands – she had admitted so herself. His foolish father had destroyed his own livelihood and his wife was a nag and a shrew. This was all her fault. She'd been the dissatisfied one. They'd all been content before she'd come into their lives.

'Growing angrier, Dyso dropped the reins and hurried home. With every step his fury grew until he didn't even feel unwell anymore. Petuna wasn't in the house, but his father directed him down to the river.

'Dyso found his wife by the water's edge and caught hold of her. He shook her with some vio-lence and accused her of consorting with witches and being the downfall of them. Petuna sobbed and sobbed, saying that she hadn't, it was all a lie. But Dyso pressed her to tell the truth, and finally she did. She wasn't the daughter of a rich man in the next village. She was Wurgrot's daughter and the woman had promised Petuna anything her heart desired. Petuna hadn't realised there would be a price to pay when her wishes were granted.

'"Of course there is a price!" Dyso howled. "There is always a price to be borne when you bargain witches, you foolish girl." And he thought of his ruined family and how none of them would ever be the same again, and how one mustn't suffer a witch to live, and he pushed Petuna into the water and jumped in after her, holding her under the water until she struggled no longer.'

This time I just stared at Raufo when he had finished. The silence stretched over the crackle and pop of the coals. I'd half expected the tale to have a grim ending like the tale of Pollixia and her tragic demise, but to actually hear it end was very different than the half-expectation.

Raufo took a swig of water from the skin, and went on. 'Jaseen looked at the enraptured king and knew that if she could begin another story before he slept, her life would be ensured for another day. So she began.

'One day long ago lived a girl named Briessa. She lived in the woods with her three aunts and was never allowed to go into town. But her voice was so sweet and her nature so gentle that she was never lonely. Robins sang on her windowsill and the squirrels bounded after her when she walked among the trees of the forest. But still she was lonely with just her aunts for company, and as she grew into a young woman she chafed beneath their strange rules. She was allowed no clothes of wool, which made the winters cold. She mustn't ever speak to strangers, though no one came to call. And most important of all, she must never, ever leave the woods.

'Her aunts told her the kingdom's legends to amuse her, and Briessa's favourite was the tale of a queen whose baby son was cursed by a wicked hag. The brave queen vowed to undo the curse, and disappeared with her ladies in waiting. No one knew where they'd gone and the king was heartbroken. But the curse never came to pass and the prince grew up handsome and strong and happy.

'Briessa thought that it would be a very wonderful thing to love someone like the handsome prince, and she believed the queen to be very courageous for finding a way to break the curse and keep him safe.

'One day Briessa was gathering berries by the brook when she came across a beautiful lady in a pale blue gown, weeping atop a smooth rock. Briessa was startled when she saw the woman, but her heart ached to see such sadness. Still, she knew the rules about strangers and began to turn away.

'But the weeping woman cried out, "Oh, my son, my prince, am I never to see you again?" The phrase reminded Briessa so much of the tale of the queen and the prince that she was rooted to the spot.

'The woman looked up and saw Briessa, and smiled so sweetly through her tears. "Hello, my child. What is your name?"

'"I'm not supposed to speak to strangers," Briessa said.

'The woman laughed. "But I'm not a stranger. Everyone knows me here: I am the queen, the prince's mother, who has banished herself to prevent the prophecy of his death."

'Briessa's eyes grew wide. "But that is just a story my aunts tell me!"

'"Nay, child. For who is it that sits on the throne, and who will succeed him?"

'Briessa thought a moment, and then said wonderingly, "Why, it is the widower king Harald and his son Prince Leos."

The beautiful lady clasped her hands together, eyes shining. "How I miss my dear husband and son. I wish I could break the curse that sits over his head. If I shan't, I shall never see them again." '"But what must you do?"

'"I must find an orphan girl with a nature sweet as river water and a voice as soft as rose petals. A girl who can charm the birds from the very trees and the creatures from the woods. And she must spin a bag of wool into the smoothest thread for me."

'Briessa said, 'Oh, would that I was that girl, for I am an orphan, but I have never spun wool. I haven't even touched it. My aunts are very superstitious about it I think."

'The woman smiled, indulgent. "My child, it is because they are poor that you have never touched wool. How silly that you think it is superstition.' The queen searched her face. 'Why, you might be the girl I have been searching for all this time! For your nature is sweet and your voice is soft, and look, all the little woodland creatures have gathered to your side."

'Briessa looked around and saw that this was true.

'"Will you help me break the curse?" the queen implored.

'Her aunts' voices were ringing in her head. As much as she wanted to help, it would be wrong. "No, I must go, I'm sorry," Briessa said, and began to back away. "They would be so very angry with me."

'The woman sighed just as Briessa was hurrying away. "Then my son will never know his true love. I had thought she might be this orphan girl I have been searching for."

'His true love! Could she possibly be the prince's true love? Briessa turned this over and over in her mind as ran home. Everyone knew that true loved trumped all – rules, conventions, everything. All the stories said so. Surely her aunts' rules wouldn't apply if this queen was to bring her to her true love.

'If the aunts could hear Briessa's thoughts, they might have regretted raising her on so many fairy stories. As it was, they noticed something different about their charge that evening. She was distracted and twinkly-eyed, and thrice smashed crockery on the flagged floor as she washed up.

"'Fie, miss! Look to your head, for it knows not what your hands are about," said the eldest aunt.

'Briessa muttered her apologies, then asked the question that had been bothering her. "Aunts, why is it we have so many pretty plates in the cupboard and plenty of food to eat, and yet we have no wool?"

'The aunts were stunned by such a queer question. "Why do you want to know?"

'Briessa looked thoughtful and they could tell she hadn't heard the question. "Is it because you three don't know how that you have never taught me to spin? It can't be because we are poor. We don't seem so poor."

'All three women went white. Each looked at the other two out of the corner of her eyes, too shocked to speak.

'Finally the youngest said, "Go to bed, child. It grows late."

'Briessa was so full of the notion of true love and how one might spin wool that she didn't notice it wasn't even her bedtime, and she tripped up the stairs to bed.

'The three aunts huddled together in conference. "Someone has been talking to her!" said the eldest.

"'Yes, she has been out of the woods and into a village," said the middle aunt.

'"It does not matter where she has been," said the youngest. "She must know about the prince. All is lost!"

'"Not yet," said the middle aunt, reaching for their largest, pointiest knife. The newly sharpened edge glistened in the candlelight. "Not if we kill her tonight."

'All three aunts looked to the stairs, wondering if their charge had had enough time to fall asleep.'

Raufo looked at me and chuckled. 'Ye're eyes are as round as that Briessa's was when she saw the beautiful lady in blue.'

I was clutching the blanket that covered me. 'Her aunts aren't going to kill her, are they? What sort of fairy story is this?'

Raufo shrugged. 'Tis a story, no more and no less. Now, off to sleep wi' ye.' He hadn't yet tied me up for the night and came forward to do it then. Without complaint, I held my wrists out to be bound. Where there was usually nothing remarkable about his expression while he bound me, his lips compressed into a thin line, as if he was reluctant to do it.

For a moment I wondered what that meant, but then cast those thoughts from my mind. I didn't care what Raufo thought. Taking this journey or not, entering Lharmell or not – it didn't matter to me one ounce.

CHAPTER EIGHT

'The aunts, the middle-born in front holding the knife, ascended the stairs towards the fair Briessa's bedroom.'

It was night again, and Raufo was continuing his tale.

'Now, you may wonder why the aunts chose to take the baby Briessa in as a baby and tend her and love her all these years, only to kill her the moment she broke their rules. But the truth is that neither were the aunts her aunts, and nor did they love her. The truth can be found hidden in the fairy stories the women told Briessa. The "middle child" was actually the queen, and the two others her ladies-in-waiting, and they had disappeared when the queen was told the prophecy that her son should perish attempting to rescue a fair maiden from a wicked hag. Discovering that fair maiden was Briessa, a princess in a nearby kingdom, the queen stole the child and chose to live in seclusion with her and her ladies-in-waiting and prevent the pair from ever meeting.

'The queen didn't want to kill Briessa, but had steeled herself that she might have to one day if her plan to keep the pair apart failed. And it seemed that day had come.

'She was inside Briessa's bedchamber, leaning over the girl's sleeping form with the knife in her hand, when the door to the cottage was flung open and they heard the sound of someone rushing into the house.

'"It is the hag! The hag!" the ladies-in-waiting cried, and shrank in terror against the wall. The queen, who had more self-possession than her ladies, hid behind the door. A cloaked figure entered, sword drawn, and the queen leapt out and stabbed the intruder through the heart.

'Briessa awoke, and sat up to see the deathly white face of a handsome young man. He was sprawled across her bed, dead.

'The queen let out an almighty howl of despair for she recognised her son. He'd perished, just as had been foretold, rescuing a fair maiden.

'Outside in the woods, the beautiful woman in the blue gown turned back into her true form, that of a wicked fairy. She smiled a cruel, pointed smile, and slunk away into the trees.'

'Wicked woman,' I mumbled into the blanket, meaning the queen. 'She deserved her punishment for stealing Briessa and trying to kill her.'

'Oh, aye,' said Raufo, in his sardonic way. 'And should she not try to protect her son?'

I sniffed, eyes closing. 'She should have tried something less heartless.' I frowned. 'All your stories are of terrible failure, Raufo. Why is that?'

He was silent a long moment and I was tempted to open my eyes to check that he hadn't dropped off to sleep himself.

Finally he answered. 'There are stories and there are stories. But perhaps now ye're ready for a different sort of tale.'

Snuggling deeper into the blanket, I said, 'Good. What's next?'

He chuckled. 'Nay, it will keep till tomorrow. Ye're nigh on asleep already.'

My voice was heavy with sleep. 'But the king will chop Jaseen's head off if she doesn't start another tale before morning.'

'Nay. Tonight Jaseen is safe. I promise.'

'This is a tale of great courage,' said Raufo the next evening.

I was sitting up on my pallet, eager for this new sort of story. The day had been much the same as all the ones that had come before it; walking beside the donkey; freezing fingers; and always, always the yearning for those little bottles of oblivion.

But despite this, the day had felt different. When I'd awoken I'd stretched – and found Raufo had forgotten to bind my wrists before I'd slept. He'd come back to the fire after doing his exercises and begun to break camp, and at any moment I'd expected him to remonstrate with himself over his carelessness. But he'd said nothing.

And, perhaps most surprising of all, I wasn't angry that I'd lost an opportunity to escape.

Warmed by the crackling fire and heaped with blankets, I listened to Raufo's tale of courage. It was about a young woman from a good family who went to live in a foreign land and take care of the king's children. She was of a fashionable foreign style, and the king wanted his sons and daughters to learn all her nation's ways so that they would have every advantage in the world. The woman liked her charges very much, but found the king to be barbaric and stubborn. Conversely, he found her to be biddable and a bore.

But over time, this meek woman showed herself a match for the king. When he was unreasonable, she told him so. When he was cruel, she stayed his hand. They began to admire and respect each other, and the king learned the power of mercy and forgiveness.

Raufo said, 'The people of the kingdom grew happy, and the woman found she was falling in love with –'

'Wait,' I said, interrupting. 'You tell me tales of sadness and death and failure, and then when I ask for a change you tell me stories of *love*?' I nearly spat the word.

'Ye don't enjoy stories of love?'

Hot anger was burning in my chest. 'You told me this was a tale of courage. I was expecting battles and heroes.'

'Sometimes it can take great courage to love. This little woman has dared to love a king. An undeserving king at that.'

I saw that he meant to go on. 'Finish it quickly and start another,' I ordered.

Raufo snorted. 'Aye, *princess*,' he sneered, and something mocking in his tone made my heart thump painfully in my chest. 'I suppose I must afear you'll cut my head off if I don't please ye.'

I threw the blankets over my head and turned away from him. 'Don't bother,' I said. 'I don't want to hear anymore tonight.' There was a wobble in my voice.

'Ah, chit,' he muttered. 'I didna mean to make ye cry. What's got into ye?'

'I don't like your story, is all.' Because it made me think of him. And that mocking address, *princess* – oh, that was Rodden all over. He never did let me forget the difference in our stations. But then, he had dared to love me. He'd been a boy from the desert, once. A glassblower's apprentice. It must have taken courage to love a Brivoran princess, though he hadn't owned it until it was too late. I'd have given anything to hear him call me *princess* or your *highness* again. To tease me. Make me annoyed and then let me see the twinkle of a smile in his blue eyes so that I would know he was deliberately provoking me. I must have been lonely if I craved even that.

Everything was so strange. I was returning to Lharmell without him, and to be welcomed rather than hated and killed. It was too incredible to believe.

Raufo finally spoke, and I could hear the regret in his quiet words. 'Will ye forgive me if I tell ye no more tales of love?'

'What do you care if I forgive you or not?' I muttered.

He gave a strangled sigh. 'I haven't the first idea, chit.'

I must have stayed silent so long that he thought I'd fallen asleep or was ignoring him, as I heard him lie down beneath his blankets. For some confounding, frustrating reason, I felt sorry for him. It wasn't his fault that I was so wretched. When he was settled I found myself saying, 'I do forgive you, Raufo.'

'Thank you,' he whispered back.

My eyes clouded with tears again, and I didn't know why.

'Do ye mind if I finish the tale of the meek little woman and the king, or shall I start another?'

It had been a long, tiring day. I hadn't managed to clear the grittiness of sleep from my eyes until the late afternoon, and I put it down to the fitful night I'd spent. The hours had been filled with painful thoughts of Rodden, and irritated thoughts of Raufo. Not just for the story he'd told me that had brought up so many memories, but because he had neglected to bind my wrists again. Why this should annoy me I didn't know, but I could only imagine that it was because he was beginning to trust me or look upon me as some sort of friend.

Friends with a harming? A Turned harming? I would be no such thing. Perhaps I should insist that he tie me up, or try to run away again so that he would have to.

But when I contemplated this I found I didn't want to. Despite my revulsion at being friends with a harming, Raufo didn't seem like the other Turned harmings I'd known. I liked the subtle shift that had occurred in the last few days. We were friendlier, more considerate. Stars above, I'd begun to cook most of our meals and made an effort to make what I knew he liked. My captor, and I wanted to please him. But most of all I wanted the stories he told. The soothing timbre of his voice as I drifted in that place between sleep and waking. An odd thing happened to his voice when he told stories. The harsh accent softened. Or maybe I was just getting used to his voice.

'Please finish it. I'm sorry I got so upset last night.'

'Nay, chit. I'm sorry.'

'Don't be. None of this is your fault.' I gave a wry laugh. 'Maybe I'll make you my favourite advisor once I am queen of Lharmell.' Glancing over to see if my little joke pleased him, I saw hardness in his eyes. 'What? What have I said?'

'Tis nothing. Now, the little woman and the king. Where was I? The little woman had fallen in love with the king. The day came when he was to choose a husband for his eldest daughter. She was in love with a young prince of little consequence, but he refused to give his permission for the match, and instead chose an older, widowed king who was very rich. The little woman saw the folly of this, and tried to persuade the king that he was not choosing for his daughter's happiness or even making a wise political decision, but out of his own vanity. The king refused to listen, and, rather than witness the unhappiness he was causing, the little woman left him and returned to her own land.

'Bereft, the king sunk into depression. All he could think about was the little woman who had left him, and how he loved her. Vowing to change, he saw to it that his children's' happiness came first in all the decisions he made for them. The kingdom was next: he meted out justice for all, and the land grew strong and happy. But he was still very lonely and missed the little woman. Several times he considered writing to her, begging her to return to him, but always his pride got in the way. Secretly he hoped that word of his goodness would reach her ears and she would return on her own.

'The king died, surrounded by his children and grandchildren and great grandchildren, a somewhat happy man.'

The sky was clear of clouds, and through the bare branches of the oak we lay beneath the stars shone with cold, distant light.

'I do not think much of your tales of love and happiness. Somewhat happy. What does that even mean?'

'Stories of love aren't always happy ones, chit.'

'I know that. I think she was very cruel not to return to him when she must have heard what a good king he had become.'

Raufo considered this. 'Perhaps she was afraid he might disappoint her again. Do ye not think he was brave for loving her so much he'd do anything to be worthy, even if he never got her back?'

'Brave to do what is right in the first place? That doesn't seem very brave to me.'

He laughed. 'Is that so, chit? Do ye find it easy, then, to do what's right?'

Considering this, I said, 'All right, the king was brave too. But why didn't he just go and get her and tell her that he was sorry and that he'd changed? She might have married him instead of them both being lonely for years and years.'

'Maybe he wasn't quite that brave,' he said softly.

I looked at him again. Raufo was looking down and his face was hidden, but I was sure he was feeling much more than he betrayed. 'What's your story, Raufo?'

'My story?' he asked, surprised.

'Yes. These stories you tell me of failure and of courage. They mean something to you, don't they?'

He rolled his shoulders uncomfortably. 'They are what Jaseen told the king.'

'Rot. Jaseen told the king about handsome princes and handmaidens to the gods and improving little women? If I was him I would have chopped off her head after the first night for being a bore. These aren't stories to please a king.'

'But they interest you, do they not?'

I rubbed my unbound wrists. 'Perhaps. But I was asking about you. Jaseen may have told all these tales to the king, or none. But you're choosing to tell them to me, in this order. Why?'

Raufo looked pleased. 'Your mind is strengthening, chit. It's coming back to life after all the months of poison. That's what a queen needs, a sound mind.' He nodded like a sage.

'You're manipulating me,' I accused.

He held up his hands. 'I'm merely telling stories.'

Struggling up, I said, 'You are not. You're trying to …' I reached for words that weren't there. My mind wasn't as strong as it used to be, but he was right. It was sharpening.

'Trying to what?'

'You're trying to *make me better,*' I accused. Suddenly it all made sense why he was no longer binding me. He didn't want me to think of myself as a prisoner. He wanted me to think of myself as a queen.

Raufo hooted with laughter. 'Damn me for a wicked scoundrel! Aye, mayhap I am trying to make you better, as ye say. I told ye why. Our queen will need a good sound mind. But first of all I need to get ye to Lharmell, and a right bored, sickly misery-guts is the very devil to travel with. You're a sight more pleasant of late, I can tell ye. So do ye want my stories or not?'

Furious, I glared at him. 'Yes,' I snapped. 'But don't tell me rubbish that you think I need to hear, or whatever you think you're doing. Just tell me what Jaseen told the king. That's all I need. Just stories to help me sleep. It doesn't matter what they're about, all right?'

'Oh, aye,' he said, and managed with those two syllables to make it clear that he would tell me whatever stories he saw fit. 'Shall I start another one for ye?'

'Oh, go on then,' I said. As I settled back to listen, I realised that he'd managed to completely evade my question: what was Raufo's story?

They grey sky of mid-morning grew darker.

We'd been travelling since just past dawn. Raufo had been cheerful enough, whistling at robins and knocking snow from low-hanging branches just to see it fall. A light powder had come down while we were sleeping and I'd blinked crystals from my eyelids as I'd woken.

Suddenly he stopped whistling and grew tense. I heard the ominous *whomp whomp* of heavy wings and noticed the change in light. Then they were over our heads – two dark bodies with enormous wingspans. The brants were descending on us while we were in a small clearing, wicked talons curved and grasping. On their backs were two hooded riders with swords drawn.

Harmings.

'Get under the donkey!' Raufo yelled and reached over his back in one fluid motion and pulled his two-headed axe from its holster. One of the brants emitted a long, piercing scream.

'Give me a weapon,' I called, knowing he kept knives about his person. Raufo, ignoring me, swung the axe in a wide, deadly arc. The harmings pulled their mounts back out of reach. Their swords were brandished but they had no missile weapons that I could see. Their pale blue eyes flashed to me and Raufo and back again, but they held their mounts where they were, knowing they'd have to go through Raufo to get to me.

I had no weapon and no armour to protect myself, so I had no choice but to duck under the donkey as Raufo had ordered, feeling like a fool. The donkey wasn't enjoying himself much either and I could sense from his twitching hide that he was getting ready to bolt. Hunched low, I hooked my fingers through his bridle and led him the short distance into the trees.

Turning to look at the skirmish I saw Raufo was keeping our attackers at bay with vicious swings of his axe, but he wouldn't be able to keep them back forever, as strong as he was. Once he tired the stalemate would end, and not in our favour. I wasn't feeling useful just huddled behind a tree so I looked around for something to throw. There were a few large rocks at my feet and I hefted one about the size of my fist into my hand. This, I thought grimly, was going to be a test of how much I'd really recovered. Whether I was still weak and useless, or whether our weeks of trekking had put some strength back into my wasted body.

The closest rider to me was a male, and he held the reins of his mount in one hand, dancing the bird closer and then quickly retreating.

'*Hey.*'

He turned to look, and I lobbed the stone right at his snarling face. It hit his temple with a dull thwack, and he toppled from the saddle, senseless.

The brant foundered for a moment, confused. In that second I saw a plan, fully formed and perfect in its entirety.

Even as Raufo was shouting at me to stay back I launched myself at the brant. It had just made up its mind to escape and leave its rider behind, and if I wasn't fast it would be up and gone. The reins were trailing, and despite the peril of the bird's wicked beak and lashing talons, I grabbed for them. Cowering, pulling blindly and expecting to be gashed open like a ripe plum at every step, I yanked the bird to the edge of the clearing, several feet from where I'd led the donkey. In a second I had it tethered and lunged away – just escaping before the sharp beak snapped at the air where my neck had been a moment before.

Turning to look at the fight I saw that Raufo was still holding his own against the remaining brant and rider. It was a female and she seemed less eager now. I hefted another stone, attempting to look more dangerous than I felt, and between my crude weapon and

Raufo's axe she must have reasoned that we weren't such attractive adversaries after all, and swept herself and her brant up into the sky.

Breathing hard, Raufo watched her go, and then swung the axe up over his shoulder and back into its holster. He turned to me, one hand on hip, and surveyed the scene before him. He looked at the donkey first, eyes wide and rolling in fright. Then the furious brant, hissing and snapping and straining at its tether. Then at me.

'Bleedin' arses and pig shite,' he swore colourfully. 'What did ye think ye were about? Ye were nearly killed – I saw the damn birdie try and take your head off!'

I gave a half smile, shrugged, and dropped my ersatz weapon. At the sound of the falling stone, the brant wheeled and hissed at it. Raufo turned his disgusted attention away from me and to the harming at his feet.

'Is he dead?' I asked, coming forward.

'No,' came the cold reply.

'Are you going to kill him?'

Raufo glared at me and pulled a length of rope from a pocket. I recognised the binding. 'He's one of my kinsmen, ye silly chit. Of course not.'

'He would have killed you,' I pointed out, though was glad Raufo wasn't going to kill anyone in cold blood, harming or otherwise.

'Mayhap,' Raufo agreed. 'But their first thought was to capture you, not kill me.'

I sniffed, watching him bind the unconscious harming to a tree. 'They didn't do a very elegant job. I would have used the advantage of attack from above and thrown down nets. That would have made it very easy to capture us, and no danger to themselves.'

Raufo muttered something to the effect that he wished they had because by now he'd be home. Straightening, he looked at the furious brant, which was still hissing at us. 'Now, what do ye suppose we're going to do with that?'

'Fly out of here, of course.'

He regarded me with a tight frown. 'What's that now, chit?'

I stepped forward. 'Don't you see? You let that harming escape. She's going to tell all the other harmings where we are. You'll be killed and I'll be taken.' I folded my arms. 'It's not the glorious end to this journey that you were hoping for, is it?'

'Nonsense, we'll move on.'

'On foot with the donkey? They'll find us again within a day. Within a few hours.'

Raufo glared first at the donkey, then at the brant again. 'Aye, and where do you suppose we go with this brant?'

'To Lharmell, of course.'

Raufo was stunned. 'Ye want to go to Lharmell now?'

'I'm sick of making and breaking camp over and over, and I'm sick of walking. I'm constantly cold and dirty. I just want this journey to be over.'

Raufo studied my face, and then my scrawny shoulders. I straightened, trying to look strong.

He shook his head. 'Nay, ye're not ready. We're walking for a reason, chit, and that's to get you sturdy in body and mind.'

I was hoping he would say that. 'Was that an order from Lharmell? Will whoever wants me there thank you for this long delay?'

Raufo grunted. 'Mayhap. But ye're no' to concern yourself with that.' He thrust a thumb to his chest. 'I want a strong queen, and ye're no' strong.'

'I am strong, and I can prove it.'

'Oh, aye. And how would that be?'

I shrugged, pretending to cast about for a means to demonstrate my strength. My eyes lit upon the brant, which was still hissing and plunging. 'I could fly the brant.'

Raufo scoffed at this. 'The birdie's no' a horse. Ye don't just need a good grip wi' your legs. Ye need to communicate with its mind otherwise it will tip you off several hundred feet above the ground.'

'I know that. I have ridden a brant before.'

'Then I am amazed you can suggest that ye're anywhere near ready.'

I wasn't certain if I was ready either, but I had to try. I didn't like walking until he said we could stop. I didn't want to enter Lharmell on his terms and being offered up as a prize. I had accepted that I had to go there again. I needed to see who it was who had ordered me to be captured and brought to them, and whether I truly was to be queen. There was nothing else for me. I couldn't go home to Amentia after killing Folsum. I couldn't take refuge in Pergamia either. Doubtless King Askar would be forced to hand me over to Ansengaad for retribution. I didn't want to go anywhere, in fact. I was a failure, and curiosity about what lay at the end of this journey was the only thing keeping me going. I would resist being Turned, of course, and if I was to die at the end, so be it. But it would be on my terms.

'I'll make a deal with you,' I said. 'If I can mount that brant and fly it once round the clearing we'll go to Lharmell today.'

Raufo looked smug. 'Aye, princess. Ye're welcome to try. But watch that it don't take your wee silly head off as you go.' He held an accommodating hand out towards the brant, inviting me to approach.

I took a deep, steadying breath. This was possibly one of the more foolish things I'd attempted to do. Raufo no doubt expected me to be lunged at by the bird once or twice and then give up. He could be right. But he didn't know that I had begun to feel the tors again. After months of fogginess, a vague awareness of Lharmell had become a sharp tug once more. I could feel them now.

The bird fixed me with one beady, flashing eye. It radiated fury and its wings were hunched. As I stepped forward it opened its enormous shiny beak in a warning hiss.

Be calm. Let me approach.

It took a lot of silent coaxing to make the brant relax even a little. That I had managed even that much gave me courage. It stood more quietly now, but its eyes were still wary. Promising it as many raw meat morsels as it desired, I stretched out a hand for the bridle, trying to quell visions of it taking my fingers off lest I give it any ideas.

I grasped the reins and the bird didn't object, merely shifting on its talons. Moving quickly before it could change its mind, I mounted the bird and sat astride its enormous wings. Casting a triumphant look at Raufo I could see he was suitably amazed.

Perhaps sensing this had gone quite far enough, he stepped forward, one hand out to take the reins from me. 'All right, chit, ye've proved –'

But I hadn't proved anything yet. *Up, up, up!* I called to the bird.

Its wings came out and I could feel its great muscles bunch beneath me, ready to spring into the air. The amazement on Raufo's face changed to horror as he finally realised the error he'd made. There was only this chance to get away. He would never trust me again. I flung everything that I had at the bird, pleading with it to launch itself into the sky. But Raufo must have begun communicating with the bird too, ordering it to stay where it was. I could feel ripples of confusion going through the brant.

But as strong as Raufo was, I was its rider, and the brant was used to listening to its rider. Raufo grabbed for the bridle – but it was too late. We launched into the air with a flurry of feathers and a great *whomp* of the brant's wings.

Raufo cried out in anguish, both in his mind and out loud, and I felt a surge of triumph. We flew once round the clearing so I could get my bearings. Then I found the tors and aimed for Lharmell, climbing as we went. The clearing disappeared below us and we left Raufo, the donkey and the unconscious harming behind. He would have to move quickly if he wanted to avoid the harmings that would undoubtedly be coming to capture me. But then, they wouldn't be his antagonists now he no longer held me captive.

It was an overcast day, but the clouds were broken up in the distance, letting some thin, mottled sunlight through. It was very cold several hundred feet above the ground, the wind hurtling past me, and my eyes were slitted as I searched the skies around me. They were empty. Below, the grey, barren forest stretched for miles. Here and there were patches of white where snow lay sprinkled upon the ground. Lharmell was many, many miles to the north, and I leaned forward to bury my face into the brant's warm, feathered neck. There was no fury in its mind now. I was taking it home.

CHAPTER NINE

Talons thudded against the earth. The brant cocked its head this way and that as if listening warily, perhaps sensing my own caution. The light was dusky within the tors, the ring of mountains shutting out much of the light left in the day. Not a creature seemed to be stirring in the barren woods, and the air was very cold. Finally, straining muscles winning out, I swung a leg over and dropped from the saddle. The bird sidled, and before I could grab for the bridle it hunched its wings and took off. Flying low it disappeared among the trees and rocky outcrops, perhaps heading for home.

It had taken several nervous days for us to reach Lharmell. I'd expected chase and capture at every moment, and had slept poorly and eaten what little I could steal from lonely cottages. But by some miracle I'd not spotted or been spotted by any harmings.

Shivering, I set out after the brant, expecting that it wouldn't be long until I stumbled across a harming, or perhaps a Lharmellin. I didn't have anything except the ragged clothes I stood up in. This was how so many un-Turned harming arrived in Lharmell. Cold, bewildered, and alone.

The tors loomed over me, blue-black and craggy. There were little caves or hollows at ground level, but it was impossible to tell from there how deep they might be. Any of them might take me underground. My memory of the last Turning underground was a blur. Not long after arriving, Rodden's old schoolmaster, Levin Servilock, had had me dosed with laudanum. I'd woken to find Rodden being beaten, and witnessed him Turning as the voices of the Lharmellins had reached their crescendo. I would never forget the feral look on his face. Changed beyond recognition, some small part of him remained, enough to fight off the Lharmellin blood for a short while. Just long enough to get me outside to safety before going back in and letting himself die in the tunnels we'd poisoned with yelbar gas.

It had never occurred to me to be grateful to him for what he'd done. How disappointed he'd be if he could see what had become of me since. But I wasn't hiding anymore, and I wasn't destroying myself a little at a time each day. I was here, in Lharmell. There was someone here I had to find.

I can't have been walking for more than a quarter hour when I came upon a trio of harmings. They were warmly cloaked and tending to a clutch of young brants and their mother. I don't suppose dirty, ragged strangers were an unusual sight to them. They looked back to the brant chicks, pretending they didn't see me.

'More bother than their worth,' muttered one to another.

'Excuse me, please.'

There was a heavy sigh, and one of them turned to face me. 'What d'you want?'

I didn't like the self-important way he thrust out his chin at me. 'Not what. Who.'

A girl, looking sounding less certain than her friend, said, '*Who* do you want?' There was suspicion in her eyes, as if she recognised me. She very well could.

I shrugged. 'I haven't the first idea. I was hoping you'd tell me.'

The third harming, a boy of about fifteen, gasped. 'It's her – it's the traitor!'

The girl thumped his arm with her fist. 'We're not calling her that anymore, remember?'

'Still a murderer,' muttered the first, casting me a dark look.

'Who brought you?' asked the boy. 'Oh, I wish it had been me. There have been so many search parties heading out every night to look for you. How clever you must have been to evade them.'

'Arse kisser,' muttered the first.

The girl looked embarrassed. 'Shut up, the both of you.' She looked at me again, wary but interested at the same time. 'Who did bring you?'

I put my hand out to the mother brant and coaxed her over to me with my mind. She stooped her great head and I ran my fingers over her soft feathers. 'No one. I came by myself.'

The girl turned to the older boy she said, 'Get Servilock.'

I watched his back as he hurried away, my hand dropping from the brant.

'You know him, don't you?' the girl asked, her expression sly.

'Yes,' I managed to say. But I had assumed that he was dead along with all the other harmings who had been at the Turning that day. Had I journeyed all this way only to find Levin Servilock at the other end? He was a particularly cruel harming, and could only want me dead, not make me queen. I turned and hastened back into the trees.

'Where are you going?' called the girl, a little laugh in her voice.

They didn't come after me. But something was. I still couldn't get my bearings in this place and didn't know if I was running into danger or from it. Finding the mountain pass out of the tors was no good. I needed another brant. Turning towards the caves again I began searching the indentations for the giant birds.

'You've come so far. Do you wish to leave so soon?' said a heavily accented voice, rasping slightly. It had emanated out of the darkness. I stepped back into the dusk light, eyes unable to penetrate the gloom. I didn't want to be a coward, and I told myself I wasn't afraid of him. But I was. He had taken everything from me, and even now, when I had nothing left to take, I was still afraid. Still backing away, I searched the pockets of darkness at the base of the tors with my eyes. 'Where are you? Show me where you are.'

The voice when it spoke held a smile. 'There, I knew you would have questions. But is that all?'

'Why did you call me here? What do you want with me?'

Something moved. There was the sound of fabric slipping across stone. 'Are those your only questions, your highness?'

If you are alive, what happened to Rodden?

He showed himself then, not where I expected to see him but several dozen feet to my left. Heavily robed with the hood up, face in darkness, the tall, imposing figure walked slowly to me.

'That's far enough,' I said, panic giving an edge to my voice.

He stopped. His hands came up and pushed the hood back. I knew that face with its broken nose and lined features. It had been sallow the last time I'd seen it, but now it was red and roughened in places, like Raufo's had been.

'Yes,' he said, noticing my searching eyes, 'you are appreciating your work. Many of us bear these scars.' He held out his hand. 'Come, we shall talk.'

'I'm not going anywhere with you. Just tell me why you went to all this bother to get me here. Was it just to kill me? How are you still alive?'

'If you stay out here I suppose you will never know.' He turned and disappeared into the gloom again.

Coercion only made me stubborn. Force would cause me to lash out. But curiosity could make me biddable as a lamb. Unable to see anything except the outline of his shoulders I followed him into what seemed like a tunnel. I found the edge of one wall and traced my fingers along its roughly hewn edge as we walked.

'Keep up, girl,' he called as I began to lag.

'It would help if there was some light.'

'There'll be light.'

Presently the tunnel did begin to brighten. We came to a torch in a sconce, and he pulled it down from the wall with one long, heavy forearm. We continued walking. The tunnel had a downhill gradient and twisted this way and that. There were forks and he chose the way as if by instinct. I tried to keep track but there were too many turns. An astounding number, in fact. I had no idea that there was such a huge underground network beneath the tors. The air was stale and heavy. I felt as if we were very, very far underground.

The tunnel widened, and became a dead end. I felt a stab of alarm – had I been brought down here in the dark only to be murdered? But it wasn't a dead end. There were, unaccountably, a set of double oak doors barring the way. They looked heavy, and were scarred with age. As we approached they swung inward. Flanking each door, standing to attention, were two haphazardly liveried stewards. Their uniforms seemed to be made out of rough homespun, but I could see what the maker had been trying for, though their skill with a needle was something to be desired.

'In there,' Servilock said, shoving me forward. 'He'll be with you soon,' he added with a laugh. Then the man retreated back up the tunnel, and despite all I knew about him I was almost sorry to see him go.

The stewards stood to attention, blank faced and unresponsive. Beyond them the cavern opened even wider into a sort of reception area. It was, I realised, a rather shabby approximation of a great hall which one might find in a castle. But nothing matched. Not the tapestried on the walls, which showed various hunting scenes or panels from great battles, but were missing the preceding or following panels. Not the carpets on the floors, which were in differing states of wear and in clashing shapes and colours. There were three tarnished coats of arms on the walls, all from Brivoran houses that I recognised but which had no association with each other. There was dusty plate and some dented suits of armour on display.

It was such an odd scene to be confronted with considering where I was that I quite forgot to wonder whom I was waiting for.

'You are Princess Zeraphina.' The voice was crisp and calm. It was a statement, not a question, and I turned to the voice. There was a man standing by a green marble column which was supporting nothing but air.

'But I don't know who you are,' I said.

He wore clothes that might have been fashionable in Brivora two decades ago. They fitted him poorly, as if he had grown quite stout since he'd last worn them. The black hair on his head was receding and fell behind his ears in short, loose curls. His face might have been handsome once, but his features were now craggy with middle age, and he bore tell-tale swollen veins in his temples. His irises were penetratingly, brilliantly blue. One side of his mouth quirked in a regretful smile. 'Do you not.'

It wasn't a question, so I didn't answer. Whatever I had expected, it wasn't this. In fact, I was rather angry with him. 'What was the purpose of me coming here? I don't know you. Are you going to tell me that you've watched me from afar, that you've studied me with great interest and you wanted to meet me face to face just once before you kill me?'

The half-smile quivered, but it didn't recede.

'Did you watch my friend die? Or were you too fond of hiding down here in the dark like a worm to come to the Turning? I see that you don't have any red scars on your face.' I looked about me again at the preposterous décor. 'How long have you been living down here in this sham palace?'

'Nearly seventeen years.'

'That's oddly precise,' I countered.

'Do you know how I can be so precise?' He stepped forward, the light from the scones sparking on the tarnished gold thread in his doublet. 'You'd not yet lived a full year when I last saw you.'

That took me aback and I thought of the stories my mother had told me about how I'd become a harming. I became indignant. 'You – you were the harming that gave blood to my mother when I was sick. You're the reason I became this way.'

He considered this. 'You could say it was my fault. But I am not that harming.'

'No? Well I'm tired of this guessing game. Just tell me who you are.'

There was that faint smile again. 'But surely you must know me by now. Princess, I am Garrick. Your father.'

There wasn't much I could think to say after that. 'You're dead,' I protested finally. He raised an eyebrow, but said nothing. Staring around me, I finally exclaimed, 'What a ridiculous room! There is nowhere at all to sit.'

He led me through to an antechamber where some high-backed, upholstered chairs were gathered around an empty fireplace. It seemed like it was just for appearance. The smoke wouldn't be able to escape anywhere, after all.

I sat, and his eyes grazed the ragged hem of my shirt, and I muttered, 'We had to keep to the forest roads to avoid your harmings.'

'We?'

I thought of Raufo and how bewildered he'd looked as I'd flown up into the sky and away. He wouldn't get the prize he'd been hoping for now that I'd delivered myself to Lharmell. 'Nothing,' I said, shaking my head.

'Perhaps you'd to wash before dinner.'

My laugh was a short, sharp bark. 'How genteel. And should I dress for dinner? Is a state room made up for me?'

To his credit I wasn't irritating him yet. 'Yes, of course. I didn't send for you without making some preparations.'

'*Send* for me? You had me abducted.' I wasn't prepared to believe that this was my father. But it did seem like he was in charge, whoever he was.

'Not at all. You were being held captive in your mother's castle by that prince. You were emancipated.'

Your mother. 'I had already emancipated myself when your harming pulled a bag over my head.'

'I think,' he said, a touch of ice creeping into his voice, 'that it is time to dress for dinner.' He stood, and two more liveried harmings came in and stood either side of my chair. 'Take the princess to her chamber and provide her with everything she requires.'

Filthy and tired and eager to get away from him, I allowed the pair to escort me. They took me to a small, neat room with a comfortable bed and more mismatching tapestries on the wall, and eventually brought hot water for a bath, though it took a long time. Stars knew where they heated it. There couldn't possibly be a fire so far underground. As I undressed, I shivered. The stone all around made it very cold.

But the water was hot and clean and I sank into it with a sigh that couldn't have been more appreciative. There were weeks of grime all over me; under my nails and in my hair. I hadn't seen the bristly end of anything in a long time. One bath didn't make me feel absolutely clean, as I got the water very murky, but by the time I stepped out of it I was vastly improved.

Garrick had indeed made preparations. There were clean under things and clothes in a trunk, and I dressed warmly in heavy skirts and a large shawl. There were good clothes in that trunk. I would take some with me when I left.

Outside my door waited the liveried stewards, and when I stepped outside they wordlessly escorted me along the passages. I would be biddable for now. I would listen to this man who called himself my father, and find out why he changed the order to kill me on sight to bring me to Lharmell and crown me.

A larger reception room, decorated in the same eclectic Brivoran style as the rest of the caverns, had a table laid for dinner. Garrick was seated at one end of the yellowed linen tablecloth. I was directed towards the other. Surreptitiously examining him I thought I could see some resemblance to the portrait that hung in my mother's castle. There was also something of Lilith about the shape of his face, though both Lilith and I had our mother's eyes. But perhaps the resemblance was only perceived. I had no proof that this man was who he said he was.

'Why did my mother tell us you were dead? Was she ashamed?' I asked the question as if I really believed him.

He had both fists laid on the table. 'Possibly. Or she believed I was dead.'

'It wasn't very kind of you to let her think so, if that was the case.'

'There is little time for kindness when one has been called upon to do great things.'

Even in my warm clothing the chill from the rough-cut stone walls was seeping into my bones. Everything I touched felt slightly damp, and a musty smell hung in the air. 'If you mean that skulking deep underground like a worm all these years is your highest achievement then I think little of your "great things".'

The fists bunched a little tighter. 'I am king of Lharmell.'

'What does this place need of kings? Since when did it even have kings?'

'When I came to Lharmell there had been nothing but hundreds of years of squalor. Look at all I've managed to achieve.' He cast admiring eyes around the hall

'When you came you must have known that the Lharmellins were slowly freezing the life out of Amentia and had been for decades. And you didn't stop them.' Rodden had discovered the reason shortly before I'd arrived in Pergamia and met him. There was yelinate in the mountains of Amentia, one half of the poison that could kill harmings and Lharmellins.

'No, I didn't,' he agreed. There wasn't an ounce of shame on his face.

'But it was your home,' I said.

'It was your mother's home, now, and then. I was her husband but she made it clear who ruled Amentia. I can't imagine she's changed much.' There was a questioning quirk to one eyebrow, and his tone was dry.

'No,' I agreed. 'No, she hasn't changed.'

Garrick gave a knowing nod. 'So you see, this is my home, as it will be yours.'

The stewards brought in clear soup, and poured cups of blood from a flagon. There was a familiar tang rising from the cups. Stomach turning, I pushed it away from me. I wouldn't make that mistake again. It was human blood, from someone strung up to drain like a butchered carcass. Garrick noticed but ignored my gesture.

'This will never be my home,' I said, trying the soup. It was surprisingly fine.

He gave a little shrug, as if to say *As you say*. But there was a smug look in his eyes that told me he didn't believe me. 'You will find that you will appreciate things differently in time, daughter.'

I was about to open my mouth to rebut this when I noticed a strange thing. The steward had left the room, but there was movement in the doorway. It seemed as if someone was pressed close to the wall, but the lighting was so dim I couldn't tell if it was a discreet servant, or something else. Garrick lifted his cup of blood, saying something lofty that I didn't catch, unaware of the movement behind him.

There was a flash of orange in the darkness. My mind still wasn't putting two and two together – yelbar, down here? Then the shape in the corner moved. Fast. A hooded figure darted forward, the knife raised in a filthy hand.

I wasn't in the habit of defending harmings, but if this harming was my father I had only just discovered he was alive. I wanted to argue with him. I wanted to know what he'd done all these years, and why. And if anyone was going to kill him at the end of all that it was going to be me.

I leaped up from the table, the chair pushing out from under me and clattering onto its back. The intruder was several feet from Garrick and he – the figure was tall and broad like a man – kept his sights on my father with single-minded purpose. Garrick gazed at me in surprise, the cup halfway to his lips. Finally the movement at his elbow caught his eye and he turned his head. He reared back in shock, but it was too late. The figure pulled back the knife, ready for the downward strike.

From four feet away I launched myself through the air, straight at the intruder's chest. We collided, the force knocking us both back and away from the table. Whoever it was was solid. Heavy. I recognised the grunt of discomfort and irritation as we fell to the floor. Landing hard on his back with me on top of him, Raufo had the wind knocked out of him. Garrick was yelling for his guards.

'Raufo, you dolt! What are you doing?' Raufo was meant to be delivering me to Garrick, not murdering him. I pulled on the lapels on his shirt and his head came up. But though they were Raufo's clothes it wasn't Raufo I was looking at. The hair was shorter and the nose smaller. His face was still reddened and rough from the yelbar gas but a lot of grime had been washed away to reveal high cheekbones, a clean-shaven jaw and a scowl as dark as a thunderstorm. It was the face of a dead man.

Shocked, I let go. The guards pulled me to my feet, and then him. He stared at me, accusation in his eyes.

'Your highness,' Rodden said, bowing his head. His words were acerbic.

For a few moments I was blank with shock. I was vaguely aware of Garrick standing somewhere nearby, and heard the order for the guards to let me go. I was released, but I could only stare, dumbfounded.

Rodden was still held by the guard's heavy hands and breathing hard. He looked between Garrick and the hall itself and then back to me, fury burning in his pale blue eyes. Rodden was Raufo. Raufo was Rodden. He'd never been dead. He'd been with me all along. He'd travelled alongside me for weeks, telling me stories and putting on that stupid accent.

He'd asked me about him. Watched me grieve for him, and said nothing. He'd just told his stupid stories and let me go on thinking he was dead.

'You bastard!' I snarled, and launched myself at him.

CHAPTER TEN

The guards grabbed hold of me and forced me back to my room. I fought them every step of the way, straining to see where the other guards were taking Rodden. The look on his face when I'd gone for him had been very satisfying. It had changed from scornful to alarmed in a flash. But it wasn't as satisfying as pummelling the stuffing out of him was going to be.

'Don't you dare kill him, Garrick,' I yelled over my shoulder as we approached my room. 'I'm going to kill him myself!' They shoved me inside and locked me in. I hadn't even realised the door had a lock. There was a single light burning in the stuffy confines.

I thought back a few days hence when Raufo had called me *your highness* even as I had been wishing I could hear Rodden say those words again. And I hadn't known it was him. How could I not have known?

'Let me out,' I cried, beating on the door. 'I'm going to be your queen, let me *out*.' But if my orders fell on any ears, they were deaf ones. Finally, exhausted and with bruises on the heels of my hands, my yelling subsided. There was nothing, no good reason – I thought as I paced – for Rodden to have kept his survival a secret from me. I stopped pacing and really thought hard for several minutes.

No. No good reason. It had caused me immeasurable pain to believe he was dead, which he had seen and could have put an end to, but he hadn't relieved it.

I couldn't fathom the why, and I certainly couldn't fathom the how. But if Rodden was alive and so was Servilock it meant that all we'd achieved at the last Turning was to give a lot of harmings a nasty skin rash. The last few months were a painful waste, and I could have wept.

The evening wore into night and no one came. Every now and then I called out for someone to release me, but not even footsteps could be heard outside the door. The room grew stuffier and I considered extinguishing the light lest it burn all the breathable air and I choke to death. But the thought of being without light – any light at all, in this subterranean tomb – filled me with dread. Eyes growing grainy, I slept. But only fitfully, and I was instantly awake many hours later after many other awakenings at hearing a key grating in the lock.

Sitting up on the bed I saw Garrick standing in the doorway. He looked rested and calm. Not like someone who had stayed up all night to interrogate an intruder, but I didn't know him well. Perhaps he had.

'Is he dead?' I asked

'He's imprisoned,' came the reply. Garrick frowned. 'Is that a relief to you?'

'Can I see him?'

He considered this for a moment. 'I am not sure that's wise just at the moment.'

'I won't kill him. I know I said that, but I was angry then,' I said, struggling to conceal my fury. 'I'm fine now.'

'If you don't want to kill him, why do you want to see him?' He smiled that half-smile of his. 'I am touched, by the way, that you should feel so protective of me.'

'That's not why I want to kill him,' I growled. 'Wanted,' I corrected. 'I just want to ask him …' I was suddenly at a loss.

'You want to ask him why, perhaps?'

What had Rodden told him about us? Garrick's expression was inscrutable. 'Yes. I suppose I do.'

Garrick stood aside. 'Very well. One of the guards will escort you.'

Garrick's artificial palace had its own dungeon even further underground. The cells were alcoves in the rock walls, only a few feet deep, and barred from floor to ceiling. All were empty but one.

'You can go,' I bade the guard who stood at my shoulder, and he left me.

Rodden was sitting on a dirt floor against the rear wall of his prison, his arms resting atop his bent knees. He was a little roughened up in places. A bruised cheek. A bloodied lip. His eyes followed my every step, taking in my heavy skirts and the warm shawl wrapped around my shoulders. It was chilly in the dungeon, and I noticed the way he had his knees drawn up to preserve his warmth.

'Sleep well, princess?' he asked finally.

The bed had been comfortable, beyond any comfort I'd felt in weeks, but my mind had been anything but comforted. 'No. I did not.'

He looked like he didn't believe me. 'What, despite all that your master has provided you?'

His derision made me want to dash the shawl from my shoulders onto the ground and stomp on it. But what would be gained from that except to prove his words had needled me? I had accepted clothes and hospitality from Garrick, but that didn't make me complicit in his actions.

'Such a friendly little scene I came upon last night,' he continued.

'He's not my *master* –' I started to say.

'Dinner, candlelight. Quite friendly indeed.' Rodden smiled, but it was not a nice smile at all.

This wasn't how this was supposed to go. I was angry with *him*. I needed answers from *him*. Not accusations. 'Is there nothing you need to explain? No deceit that you need to admit to?'

He got up, a little stiffly, and pressed his face close to the bars, hands gripping them tightly. 'Why did you protect that man? You escape on a brant and fly straight to Lharmell, and when I pursue you, thinking I am rescuing you, I see you with that man at dinner.' He said 'dinner' like it was a foul thing.

'I don't need rescuing,' I snapped. 'I wanted to enter Lharmell on my own terms, not as a prisoner. I was sick of being a prisoner – your prisoner.'

'How long have you been lying to me? All through the night I have been trying to think of a reasonable explanation why you would stop me killing him when I had the chance. He's the one who's been controlling things, don't you realise? He's the one we've been fighting all along.'

'I know that,' I said tightly. The hypocrisy of it, that he would like awake wondering how long I'd been lying to him.

'Then why, Zeraphina?' His knuckles were bloodless and white where they gripped the bars.'

I stared at him. 'Weren't you listening? Were you so intent on murder that you didn't hear a word we were saying?'

'No, I didn't hear anything. It didn't matter what he was saying, or you were saying, because that man needs to die.'

At some point I realised I'd accepted what Garrick had claimed. It might have been when I'd seen Rodden about to kill him, and some instinct of familial preservation had taken hold of me. Or perhaps it was when I'd realised Rodden was alive, and stranger things could happen than long-dead fathers ruling Lharmell. 'Rodden, he's my father.'

For a few moments Rodden didn't have anything to say, which I found intensely, if briefly, satisfying.

'Your father's dead,' he said quietly.

'So I thought. But it seems that some people who pretend to be dead aren't really dead after all.'

Rodden, ignoring my accusation, turned away and rubbed a hand through his hair. 'This explains so much,' he muttered, lowering himself to the floor of his cell.

'Nothing has been explained. Where is your explanation for what you have done?' I was pressed against the bars now, as if I was the prisoner and he was free.

He slumped down on the floor of his cell. When he raised his eyes they were mocking. He'd been mocking before, but now there was a cruel glint in his eyes that I'd never seen before. 'So, when can I expect the happy event?'

'What happy event?'

'Your coronation. Does being a friend of the heir to Lharmell grant me certain privileges? Oh, I know I'm only a lowly prisoner, but perhaps you might arrange for me a hot bath and some warm clothes. Before I'm executed, I mean.'

It was clear from his manner that he didn't think he owed me any sort of explanation. I was the harming's daughter and he was the prisoner. It didn't matter to him that he'd lied to me for weeks. There was nothing familiar in the hateful expression on his face. He might as well be another person. I wished he was another person. Raufo, in his way, had at least been kind to me. Most of the time.

'Go swive a goat,' I spat, and stalked out.

I avoided Garrick all day, and his summons to dinner that night. There wasn't much to do in the cold little cell that was my bedroom, but I slept and woke, and then slept some more. The journey had taken its toll on me and, despite where I was and everything that had happened, it felt good to be in a warm bed with a roof over my head again. While I was awake most of my thoughts were consumed by Rodden and Raufo. All Raufo's little mannerisms and quirks started to make sense. The voice that changed subtly as he told his tales, the accent neutralising. His obsession with that little wooden box which must have contained his false nose and bits of stick-on hair. His body had changed too. He'd never been a weakling, but he'd had the lean body of an archer. If he'd used a bow I might have known him from his stance and skill. So he'd chosen another, heavier weapon and changed his body to suit it.

Some things stayed the same. His detestation of laudanum, for instance. The first harming that had tried to bring me to Lharmell didn't much care if I was conscious or not, but Raufo had. Rodden had always had a strong dislike for the substance. The laudanum was probably the main reason I hadn't known him for who he was. With my senses dulled I hadn't detected that familiar Rodden-ness about him, in the same way I hadn't felt the tors until the end.

But the stories should have given him away. I knew all the tales of Brivora, but Raufo had told me tale from the desert, where Rodden was from.

As well as feeling very stupid about this I still couldn't fathom why he'd felt it necessary to conceal his identity from me. That he'd been taking me to Lharmell for the glory of bringing the future queen home must have been a lie. His true purpose was to kill Garrick. And I had been bait.

After a long day and an even longer night I awoke to a growling hunger in my belly. There was cold water in a ewer to wash with and I changed into clean linens and the same heavy skirt, blouse and shawl, and went to see about something to eat. There was no guard by my door so I found my own way.

The chambers and corridors were very still and silent. Garrick was nowhere to be found, and finally I asked one of the guards in the hall where he was, and was told he was above ground. Uncertain whether this was a disappointment or a relief, I ate by myself and then sat in one of the chairs by the empty grate that Garrick and I had sat in previously.

Rodden was in his cell not very far away, and I could go and see him if I chose to. But I didn't want to. Before, there had never been a time that I hadn't wanted to see Rodden. For the past few weeks I had silently begged anything and everything that might be listening to let me see Rodden just one more time. Now, though, I couldn't stomach the thought of laying eyes on him.

Finally, Garrick returned. I couldn't read the cool expression on his face, but then, I didn't know him. Perhaps he was naturally aloof, or perhaps he thought it best to be guarded around his un-Turned harming daughter.

He sat in the other chair. 'You haven't been to see the prisoner today, I am told.'

'I don't want to talk about him.'

Garrick gave a slow nod, and then steepled his fingers. 'When you are ready I will take you all around your new island home, and show you –'

'I don't want to talk about that either.'

He pressed his lips together in annoyance. 'What do you want to talk about, daughter?'

The exasperation on his face reminded me so much of my mother that I felt a pang of homesickness. I wished I'd never left Amentia and that the north had remained a smudgy memory from schoolroom geography.

'Why did you leave my mother?' I finally asked.

'I was called to greater things.'

'You had a family. You had responsibilities to us.'

His expression was wry. 'I doubt your mother had any trouble managing the pair of you. She was always more than capable, as a queen and as a mother.'

'That doesn't mean she wanted to.'

'That is all in the past, Zeraphina. It is the future we must think of.'

I didn't want to think about the future, and especially not the future he was offering. I was still trapped in the past. Imprisoned just as surely as Rodden was in his underground cell.

'How did it happen?' I asked.

'The how is immaterial. What matters is that it did, and that you were chosen, too.'

I stared at him. 'You think you were chosen? You were tricked, and my mother was too.'

'There is no trickery in being given this wonderful gift. I became someone the day I became a harming.'

'You already were someone. You were king of Amentia, and you were our father.'

He gave an impatient gesture and muttered, 'King regent. Here I am king in my own right, and I can bestow my kingdom on my daughter.'

An ugly suspicion was forming in my mind. Were these the words of a Turned harming, or was this how he'd truly felt being married to my mother – like some second-best ruler? 'Was being my mother's consort not enough for you?'

'You will understand one day when you have your own consort. He will love you and support you, but he will have no true power. You will be the valued one, and a small part of you will pity him that no one looks to him as they look to you.'

'Have you chosen my husband for me while you have been above ground?'

'Of course not. I speak of the man we are holding in the dungeon.'

I burst out laughing. 'Rodden won't be my consort. He would never consent to being forced into such a thing.'

Garrick looked genuinely confused. 'Why, of course he will. After.'

My laughter died. 'After what?'

'After you are both Turned, of course.'

I felt cold. For a moment I had forgotten who, or rather what, I had been talking with. 'We are not going to be Turned.'

'But of course you are. That is why you are here. And you want it, which is why you have come.' He gave me a thoughtful look. 'I would have thought you'd be happier to see him. Don't you see? I'm giving you a way to be together that your mother would never allow.'

It was shocking that he knew so much about us. Had Rodden told him everything, or was he simply that perceptive? For a traitorous moment my heart leapt. But it was too ridiculous to entertain, the thought of Rodden and I ruling Lharmell together instead of fighting to overthrow it. 'I have been to Lharmell twice before and both times I have ruined your Turnings. I assure you I do not want it and can't fathom how you would want me.'

'The path to great power and leadership is often fraught for those most deserving. The strength of your feeling for this place has left you confused.'

How easily he explained away my hatred for Lharmell and my abhorrence for being Turned.

'I promise you, I am far from confused.'

He smiled a small, self-satisfied smile and begged me to excuse him. I sat for a long while in the chair by the cold grate after he had left me, trying to remember all my mother had told me about my father. There wasn't a lot. He had been her equal, she had said. No doubt she'd meant her equal in mind and ambitions, for as a younger son he wasn't her equal in rank. But she'd said she'd treated him as her equal. Had she told me he was a proud man, or was that only something I was seeing now? I couldn't recall. Certainly he was proud now. And authoritarian. I didn't like that he had my life planned out for me to the letter.

Garrick had probably always been a proud man, but I doubted that my mother could have loved someone with such irritating self-assurance. Perhaps that had come after. Were you a different person once you were Turned? I'd seen it happen to Rodden, but the effects had only lasted for a few terrifying moments and he'd been able to fight it off somehow. Orrick, the first mate of the *Jessamine*, I'd known briefly before he'd been made a harming. He'd been a genial young man, but even before we encountered any harmings superstition and fear had twisted him into something dangerous. When he actually did become a harming, he despised us just as energetically for being enemies of Lharmell.

Don't you see? I'm giving you a way to be together.

We were so lost, Rodden and I. We had been fighting so long that we had turned on each other. If we somehow reconciled and continued on our path, then Garrick had to die along with all the other harmings. I didn't know if I had it in me to kill my own father.

'Where have you been?'

Rodden was huddled in the corner of his cell, dark smudges under his eyes and a snarl on his face. I pushed several blankets and some food through the bars, but he didn't move to take them so I lay them on the ground inside the cell. 'With that creature?'

'He's not a creature. He's my father.'

'That doesn't mean he's not your enemy.' There were several rats' bodies on one side of his cell. He hadn't been going without blood, then. I should probably follow his example if I didn't want to resort to human blood.

'He would let you out if you asked,' I said. Garrick hadn't promised anything of the kind, but I was sure I would be able to talk him into it.

'Harmings aren't in the habit of letting their prisoners go, Zeraphina. Come to think of it, they're not in the habit of keeping prisoners in the first place.' He looked around at the bars. 'How … *Brivoran* this all is.'

'My father is Brivoran,' I said.

Rodden gave me a sharp look. 'He's not your father.'

'Of course he's my father.' I spoke with conviction even though I'd been wondering the same thing myself not an hour hence. 'And I didn't mean he'd release you. Just let you out of this cell.'

'Ah. So you're a prisoner too.'

The truth was I hadn't tested whether I was a prisoner or not. I suspected I was, and that those heavy oak doors would be barred to me if I approached them.

'Please, Rodden. If you ask him he will release you, I'm sure of it.'

'I'd rather rot in his cells than eat at his table. I didn't mean that he's not the man who fathered you. If you say he is then I believe you. But that man is gone. He died when he was Turned.'

'You don't have to eat at his table,' I said, ignoring what he said about Garrick. 'Stars above, Rodden! I can't talk to you when you're like this.'

'Like what?'

'Imprisoned. You want me to feel wretched.'

'Do you feel wretched?'

'I do. In so many ways.'

'Good.'

'Don't be a child.'

'What do we even have to talk about?'

'Why you lied to me and let me think you were dead!'

'Don't you think it matters very little now, in the circumstances?'

'It matters to me. It is everything to me.'

This was why I wanted him to be released. So we could talk as equals face to face, not with me out here and him in there, enjoying his martyrdom. 'Why did you use me as bait?'

He was silent a long moment, and I expected the next words out of his mouth to be a flat denial. But he said, 'I suppose it must look that way. But that was never my intention.'

'What do you mean?'

'We were never meant to go to Lharmell together. I was taking you to Pergamia and I was going to leave you there while I went to find out who it was who wanted to make you queen. And then I planned to kill them.'

'Why didn't you tell me that as soon as we were alone? I can understand your disguise if it was for the benefit of the harmings that might find us. But why did you disguise yourself from me?'

'I was going to tell you. Then you were so ill and I … Well, I thought I would tell you as soon as you were stronger. I was going to tell you before we reached Pergamia, at any rate.'

Rodden had always had a habit of keeping things from me, consciously or unconsciously. He was a naturally guarded person, and when he'd finally brought me into his confidence about what had happened when he was a boy in Verapine I thought I'd breached his tight wall of secrecy. That I was trusted. But it seemed not. 'I thought the days of you keeping things from me were long over.'

He winced at that, but repeated, 'You were so unwell. I barely knew you.'

'You saw how wretched I was, thinking you were dead. But you just told me silly stories and pretending to be someone else.'

He looked up, eyes filled with scorn. 'Think back to how you were when I came upon you in the back of that cart. Would you have trusted you?'

'Whose fault was it that I was in such a state? I felt you die, Rodden. Do you know what that did to me?' It had seemed so real, the orange poison eating away ay him. Snapping the thread between us.

'I do. It was probably very much like how I felt as I lay in Lharmell, too ill to move after having been poisoned by our own trap, and not knowing what had become of you. Not knowing –' He gave a helpless gesture and closed his mouth.

It hadn't occurred to me that he'd worried that I was dead, too. But that made his lies all the worse if he knew how terrible it felt. 'Why aren't you dead, anyway?'

'Try to sound a little less disappointed, would you?'

'I mean, what was wrong with the yelbar preparation? Didn't the alchemist mix it correctly?'

He let out a long sigh. 'I've had a long time to think about that. Do you remember me telling you that the yelinate from the Amentine mountains looked different somehow?'

'Yes. Darker wasn't it, like it was impure?'

'Something like that. I don't know what was wrong with it exactly, but it didn't work like we expected it to. Instead of dying, it seems that the Turning was reversed for everyone who was there, though it made everyone very sick and gave us terrible burns where our skin was touched by the vapour.'

I wanted to say how glad I was that it hadn't killed him, and how sorrowed I was by the pain he'd endured, but anger kept those words unspoken.

'The burns did serve one purpose,' I said.

'What was that?'

'They helped to disguise you as Raufo.'

Rodden's voice was bitter. 'I wish you wouldn't think about that. Don't think about anything except finding that knife I brought into Lharmell, and killing that creature with it.'

CHAPTER ELEVEN

That night I ate dinner with my father.

It was all so easy for Rodden. He got to sit in his cell, his self-satisfaction to keep him warm along with the blankets that I'd given him, absolved from making any decisions. While I, on the other hand, had try and make a decision: father, or monster?

'There is so much I want to show you now you are here, Zeraphina,' Garrick said, pushing his plate away and sitting back. He raised the corners of his mouth in a small smile.

'Is there?'

'Indeed. I can show you how everyone and everything on this island serves the great purpose of Lharmell. The harmings can greet you and pay homage.' He leaned forward. 'You can discover all the secrets of this underground system. Afterwards, of course.'

'After what?'

'Your Turning, of course. You and that man in the dungeon.'

'His name is Rodden,' I said.

Garrick cast his eyes to the wall beyond me in a dismissive gesture. 'I can learn his name when he is one of us.'

'One of *you*,' I corrected. 'You seem so certain we will submit to this Turning, and yet you do little to persuade me that Lharmell is right and good and the place where I should make my home.'

'But my dear, the Turning will convince you of that. I don't need you to submit. You will be Turned whatever your feelings may be.'

I stared at him. It hadn't occurred to me that he wouldn't give me a choice in the matter. 'But I'm your daughter,' I blurted.

He raised his glass of blood. 'Indeed you are.'

'You – you're supposed to love me, and respect me and want me to be happy.'

'I want all those things.'

'But to *force* me to become your successor, and to force Rodden …'

He waited for me to finish my thought.

'You can't.'

'You will feel very differently after. How you feel now will be a distant memory. You will be filled with such love for your fellow harmings, and gratitude to the Lharmellins that they have given you the capacity for such love. Everything will make sense at last.' His smile had become almost beatific.

'But it won't be real. It won't be me. Do you even remember the person you once were? Do you have any conscience at all for the things you have done, or what people like Servilock have done in your name?'

'Why would I feel any pangs of conscience for the things I have done? I am proud of all that I have achieved in the last decade and a half. I made the harmings see that they needed a king, that they would be stronger with their own leader while still obeying the Lharmellins.' He was silent a moment. 'I could regret one thing. That I did not discover sooner that my own daughter had been brought to the fold. But here you are.' The broad smile was directed at me now, and I finally understood why he'd done little to persuade me that my place was as queen of Lharmell. He was right. He wouldn't need to persuade me. The Turning would do that for him.

'When is it?'

'When is what?'

I threw the linen napkin from my lap and onto the table, and stood. 'You know what.'

'The Turning? It will take place in three days' time. A glorious ceremony under the stars.' He smiled at me. 'We needn't be afraid of any tricks or intruders this time, after all.'

I was trapped. There was no way out. I made sure of that by roving the underground palace all the next day. Garrick refused to take me up into the open air until the ceremony. Even if I did manage to get away from him and escape, there was still Rodden in the dungeons. No matter how furious I was with him I couldn't leave him behind.

I believed Garrick that after the Turning I would feel everything he told me I would feel. Perhaps that should have been a small consolation. That afterwards we would feel no regret, and no remorse for the things we would do. But imagining us like that made me sick with horror. Over and over I saw Rodden's pinned pupils and feverish face in those moments when he'd just been Turned.

Garrick noticed my despondency at dinner and tried to lighten the mood with tales of the places he'd been, carefully omitting any mention of harmings or blood or his plans for me. He had seen some beautiful, far-flung places, but every time I felt a stirring of interest I remembered what he was and why he might have travelled, and my interest palled.

Finally he pushed his plate aside and stood. 'Come. I wasn't going to show you this until after. But there's no reason you can't see it now.'

'What?' I asked. But he merely smiled his small smile and motioned me to go ahead of him.

He directed me through the corridors, deftly turning left and right. The floor sloped downwards, and there were no sconces to light the way. He held a torch and that became our only meagre light. The air was thick and musty. Presently a sound came floating along the dark tunnel like bubbles rising to the surface of a stream. I caught snatches every few moments. Then whole melodies ran together. Voices, and they were singing.

A pale blue glow appeared ahead, growing brighter and brighter with every step. Then finally the tunnel opened onto a huge cavern, spread out beneath us. We were standing atop a balcony overlooking hundreds of Lharmellins. Perhaps a thousand or more – I couldn't tell. Their eyes were like shifting stars, beautiful, and yet cold.

'Aren't they perfect?' Garrick breathed, somewhere over my left shoulder. I nodded, and was drawn forward. The singing of Lharmellins had always captivated me.

'What are they doing?' I whispered.

'They are singing.'

'But why?'

'Listen to them. They will tell you.'

It was such a bittersweet sound that it was easy to forget all my confusion and heartache of the previous days. The music reached out to me, curling round my body in soft tendrils. I closed my eyes, the better to hear, and found that I could see the singing. It was all around me like a soft, pulsating web, rising up and outward – far beyond the walls of the cavern and out across the island. The singing was Lharmell. This was the tor-line which I'd felt my whole life. Though I had deadened it with laudanum these past months it was stronger than ever now. It earthed me to the ground like a ship docked at its home port.

The pitch of the voices rose, and I rose with them. My mind flowed outward with the ripples of sound and in my mind's eye I could see Garrick and myself as if from above. We were all connected by gossamer lines, to Lharmell, and to each other. I rose higher still and saw that a thicker line than the others ran from the centre of my chest to a place beyond the cavern. Rodden. Was this what he saw when he travelled out of his body? The cavern fell away and I saw the web racing out towards Brivora, and spreading out. Thousands of lines descended into Pergamia, and hundreds of thousands more across all the cities south across the continent. More glowing blue lines travelled west, towards Verapine. Every one of those lines was a tor-line connecting a harming to Lharmell. This was what kept them loyal, and this was what brought them home. They were linked to the very stones of Lharmell.

I sank back into my body and opened my eyes.

'Did you see?' Garrick's face was brimming with eagerness.

I couldn't speak for a moment. I was still seeing that exquisite web that connected us all. It was so strong. And so beautiful.

'I see it. I see everything now.'

CHAPTER TWELVE

'Where the hell have you been?'

Rodden was standing, breathing hard, behind the bars of his cell. There was a furious glint to his pale blue eyes that I knew well.

Looking away, I rubbed a fingertip over the rough-hewn wall. 'Nowhere far. I'm a prisoner here too, you know.'

'It's been days. I've been worried.'

I shrugged. He wasn't going to get an apology from me even if it had been days. Not knowing what to say to him was an unusual experience for me. I'd always known exactly what I wanted to say to Rodden, and I'd said it, whether he wanted to hear it or not. But if I spoke to him he might question me. And there were no answers that I could give that he would want to hear.

'I'm more of a prisoner than you are, you know. I'm locked in here, and you're out there with him,' he went on.

I wiped my fingers on my skirt and turned to go. 'I'll come to see you later. I have to go.'

'No, you won't.' He voice held an odd, desperate note. He'd reached up to grip the bars, his face close to the iron. 'I can't stand it in here. Something's going on. Something you're not telling me.'

Would it be worse, or better, to tell him that I couldn't save us? I doubted that Rodden could find peace with this knowledge while trapped behind bars. And soon it wouldn't matter whether he made peace or not. 'I'm sorry.'

'Why are you sorry? What has he been saying to you? What are you going to do?'

But I'd already taken a few quick steps and disappeared from view, his questions arrowing into my back.

Every time I closed my eyes I would see that web before my eyes, and feel all the power it possessed. It was like a living thing. This was truly the heart of Lharmell. Not a person or some rocks, or this great underground chasm itself. Lharmell was this web, and it held everyone and everything together.

It was the song that was the most beautiful. It couldn't compare to anything else. Not any taste nor any scent. It was the sweetest thing I knew, and it belonged to the most unlovely creatures in the world.

The Lharmellins were spread below me like a rolling sea, always moving, eerie eyes aglow and their open mouths full of pointed, needle teeth. I searched their faces, hungry for what they could give me. But hesitant at the same time. This was forever. I hadn't asked Rodden, and there was no way to get him out. I was sorry that he couldn't be spared, and I didn't have the words to tell him what I was about to do.

I reached out to the Lharmellins and my eyes drifted closed. The tor lines glowed in my mind's eyes. They surrounded me, a great luminous web. As the Lharmellins sang they kept the tor-lines strong and anchored them to the very heart of the mountains. Out they travelled, thousands upon thousands of them, lines of shimmering light and need, across all Brivora. Each and every one was connected to a harming, keeping him or her prisoner. Obedient. Or if they were un-Turned, the lines called them home to Lharmell for the final journey into the fold.

I hated the tor-lines. Before I knew what the pain deep in my chest meant they had brought me confusion and fear. I recalled how, before I met Rodden, I had been afraid of myself and what the strange longing for the north meant. I had been afraid of Rodden, too. Then when I knew that the line made me a slave to Lharmell I had resented it, and fought to conquer the pain and need. They had caused me so much agony and sleeplessness I couldn't imagine a life without them.

I reached out, and it was like the first time I called a wind. Not knowing what I was doing, I tested the air with my mind. I sent out mental hooks, dragging on the lines, feeling the web pull tighter. The mountains groaned. But the Lharmellins kept singing.

Did they know what they were doing with their singing? I wondered. Did they feel the quakes that reverberated through the tors?

Sing louder. Sing more.

The Lharmellins heard their future queen. The voices rose in exaltation, singing the lines tighter, thicker. All over Brivora I sensed hundreds upon thousands of harmings feel the tug and that nascent urge to return home.

Sing for your queen, I coaxed the Lharmellins.

Deep in the earth, something cracked. I felt it, and an answering twang of fear. But if I let myself be afraid I would never be able to finish. Instead, my mind went to the tor-lines, hoping they would let me see what the laudanum still clouded. Along the lines I flew till I found Garrick in his throne room, gazing at his Brivoran trappings. Hearing me say, *I see everything now.* And I did – only it wasn't what he wanted me to see. I had needed this. I had needed to be brought here to find my long-dead father alive and transformed into something ghastly. I had even needed to be betrayed by Rodden. And I had needed to be tempted to give in. Otherwise I would never had found the courage to do what I now did.

Finding the lines again I flew up and away from the creature that had once been my father. In his prison, Rodden knew something was wrong. He was on his feet, hands gripping the bars. He was listening, dark brows drawn down. He hadn't yet fathomed what was happening, but he was quick. He would in a few moments.

I was dragging the rock across the entrance, sealing myself in. Except I was shutting us both in. The earth shook beneath my feet.

Louder, I urged. *More!*

The Lharmellins sang, and the tor-lines wrenched at the mountains. Rodden had once told me that the island was an ancient spent volcano. It must lie on a rift in the earth, and where there was a rift, there was weakness. The Lharmellins had great power and control of the tor-lines, but they can't have known they were slowly tearing the island apart. It would rend in time, but not fast enough for me. If I was to prevent the Turning in a few days' time it had to happen now. There were many thousands of tons of rock above my head. If it came down, the tor lines would break and the Lharmellins would be crushed. The harmings all over Brivora would still be harmings, but they would no longer be beholden to Lharmell. There would be no new Lharmellins and no king or queen to rule them. The harmings would never feel that awful clawing in their backs. They might be thirsty, but there would be no one to teach them to be cruel with that thirst.

The mountains would fall down onto my father's head, and Rodden's. Onto all the Lharmellins who were singing like the end of the world had come. And onto me, and I would know that in the end I hadn't given up after all.

There was a loud crack, and the ground shook. Just a tremble at first, and then a great shuddering that knocked me off my feet. I opened my eyes and looked down. Everything was shaking so much it had become a blue blur, but I could still hear the Lharmellins. They were tearing Lharmell apart and still they kept singing. I pressed myself back against a rock face, silently urging them on.

Rodden must know what was happening by now. He must have heard me. I hadn't been trying to conceal my thoughts. I slid to the floor, arms wrapped around my knees, and felt the tremors coursing through the mountain. The singing was still audible over the rumbling of the earth, and still beautiful. It came and went in snatches between the fiercest tremors.

Something was coming down the passageway. It was angry and it was moving fast. It burst out into the meagre light.

'*Stop.*'

At Garrick's shout the Lharmellins fell silent, but the mountains kept quaking. He stared around him with wide, shocked eyes, one hand braced against the passage wall. His eyes found me.

'What have you done, Zeraphina?' His shock turned to anger, and he started towards me, a murderous set to his face. Dust and little particles of rock had been showering down for several minutes, and it was only a matter of time before something larger was shaken free. A particularly violent tremor surged through the rock, there was a crack, and stones began raining down. Tucking my head against my knees I covered the back of my head with my hands. The shuddering went on and on, building up to something huge. Stones pelted me, some as large as lemons, bruising my arms and legs.

There was a sound like the bones of a giant breaking. I felt the air pressure change on my skin. Finally, the worst of the shaking subsided. There was something missing, and I thought it was the singing or the quaking. Then I thought it must have been the shock that I was still alive. But then I realised. I couldn't feel the tor-line. Sending my mind wider, searching, I came up with nothing. No web. No lines.

I stood up, and then doubled over, coughing. The air was full of dust. A sconce was still burning on a far wall, and it cast wan light over a scene of destruction. Rocks had fallen everywhere. In some places small stones and rocks littered the ground, as where I sat. In others great boulders had fallen.

The Lharmellins were silent, and their eyes flashed as if they were milling about, uncertain what to do next. In places it was dark, as if many rocks had fallen there to cover them. I turned back to the passage. The entrance was still relatively clear. I could climb over the rubble and feel my way along. Possibly it had fallen in further along and I was trapped.

With each step over the rubble I looked about me. 'Garrick?' The silence answered. Edging forward, I called, 'Garrick, are you there?'

Not far from the entrance to the passage way I was starting to think he had been buried so deeply beneath the rubble that I would never find him, when a hand grabbed my ankle. I shrieked into the darkness and pulled free. The hand had gripped tightly, but gave up just as quickly, as if it didn't have the strength or inclination to hold on.

It was Garrick's hand. I recognised the shape, the prominent bluish veins on the back and the silvery hairs on his wrist. Nothing else of him was visible.

Digging him out, I didn't know what I wanted to find. I must have lifted more than a hundred rocks to uncover his torso, not knowing if I was standing on the very rocks that were crushing him. One side of him was pinned by a boulder I couldn't shift, and so were his legs. But he was alive, somehow, and after a few minutes he opened his eyes. His breathing was laboured.

'I'm sorry,' I said.

He coughed. 'No, you're not.'

My eyes filled with tears, because he was right, in a way. I wasn't sorry I'd done this thing. But I was sorry for what had become of him.

Blood trickled from his temples into his hair. 'I gave you life. I would have done it a second time over, and given you so much more besides.'

'Even though I didn't want it?'

He managed a small smile at that. A real smile, and I knew it came from some part of him that still remembered what it was to be human. 'It always was useless trying to get your mother to do anything she didn't want to do. I might have known you'd take after her.' His blue eyes when he looked at me were very pale, like they'd been leached of their vitality. 'You can go, if you like. Don't stay here with me. Find out the extent of what you've done. If you can get out, that is. There may be other rock falls.'

'I know.'

'You didn't plan on living this long, did you?'

'No.'

'Make good use of your time, then.'

'I'll stay.'

'And watch me die?'

He was a direct man. I wondered if he'd been like that before he'd been Turned. It was a quality my mother would have admired, certainly. I had spoken the truth when I said I forgave him. None of this was his fault. Perhaps he'd been a direct man before, but I was sure that he wouldn't have been a man to force his daughter into a life she didn't want. He was my father, and yet he wasn't.

'And not leave you.'

'I may be some time going.'

I doubted it. His breath was coming in short gasps, every one of them painful, and he was bleeding profusely.

'Want to be sure … I'm dead?' he wheezed. The last of the light in his eyes twinkled with something akin to amusement.

'Something like that.' I took his free hand and held it. There was no strength in it now, and his fingers were cold. We sat for long minutes, nothing but his rasping breath to fill the silence.

'It's over,' I whispered. 'I'm sorry it ended this way for you, but I'm glad it's over.'

His eyes had become fixed and his lashes fluttered. So quietly that I had to bend my ear close to his mouth to hear his last words, he said, 'No, it isn't.'

The rasping stopped, and there was nothing but silence.

The journey back up that tunnel was made in total darkness. I felt my way over rocks and around them, all the time trying to find that one thread that I desperately wanted to find. But with the tor-line had died the thread that I knew to be Rodden's; or I just wasn't able to find it without calling upon the Lharmellins for help. At least, I told myself so.

In places I had to dig my way through, lifting rocks and hurling them behind me, or scraping away falls of stones. My raw fingers began bleeding, but I didn't find myself panicking. Either there was a way through, or there wasn't. I had prepared myself not to live through my plan, so every minute longer that I lived was a revelation.

Finally, there was light.

The corridors beyond were clear of rubble and I ran now, hope that I might not die after all making me greedy. If I had made it this far Rodden must be alive too. It was only fair, I told myself, knowing that life and death had little to do with what was fair.

The closer I came to the dungeons the more rocks again littered my path, and I had to slow and pick my way over them. Every few steps I was calling to him in my mind, but could feel nothing of him. Whether this was my own failings or something worse, I couldn't tell. For him to be truly dead now would be the cruellest mischief. It would be just *like* him to do such a thing: die, just when I had the leisure to have it out with him properly about pretending to die the first time.

The entrance to the dungeons were clear, and I raced in. Spluttered accusations assaulted me the moment I entered.

'What in blazes have you done? This was you, wasn't it? We might have all been *killed* –' He was up and gripping the bars, covered in dust with a nasty cut on his forehead. His cell was a rubbly mess of rocks and dust, and the bars were bent beyond recognition by falling rocks. He'd been trying to work himself free, loosening the bars where the rocks were cracked.

'That was the idea,' I snapped. 'I wanted to destroy everything so it would finally over. Even if it meant destroying us as well. Or are you the only one who's allowed to try and get themselves killed in Lharmell?'

He looked even more furious at that. 'You might have told me. You let me think you were going to let us be Turned.'

I suppose I had let him think that, though it hadn't been my intention. I just hadn't known how to tell him that I was probably going to kill us both. '*You* might have told me you weren't dead. You only had weeks to do it.' There came the sound of far-off rumbling, and the ground shook. Only a slight tremor, like the warning growl of a wild animal. There would be worse to come.

'There's no time for that now. I don't suppose you have the key?' His voice was tight.

'No, I don't. I left it buried under rocks with my dead father.'

Some of the heat went out of his face. 'Oh. Well. I don't suppose the key would have done much good in any case. The door is bent out of shape.'

'Can we work the bars loose?'

'I've been trying that. As you can see I haven't got very far.'

I shook the bars with him. They rattled, but stayed put. They'd been sealed into place with some sort of mortar, and I thought that if we could break it away we could free the bars. There was a chunk of rock at my feet and I beat at the mortar at the foot of one of the bars. Rodden saw what I was about, took up a rock and did the same where the bar met the ceiling.

'You're getting grit all over me,' I muttered.

'I do apologise for trying to break out,' he replied, still pounding away. 'Shall I stay prisoner forever?'

'I just thought you'd like to know.'

'Because we are intimate friends?'

'Oh, shut up.'

After several minutes we'd cleared a lot of mortar out of the way and Rodden, seemingly annoyed with the slow progress we were making, grabbed hold of the bar and began yanking it back and forth in its socket. It was a lot looser now.

'Come – on – you – dratted – thing,' he said with each tug, getting even redder in the face beneath his yelbar burns. I grabbed a hold of the bar and we shook it till our teeth rattled, and then we shook some more.

'I think – it's –' I began, and then with a scraping sound it came free – 'working,' I finished.

Rodden threw the bar past me and it clattered to the stone floor. There wasn't an enormous gap for him to slide through, but he tried it anyway.

'Think thin thoughts,' I suggested, standing back and watching him press his body sideways between the bars. He had an arm and a leg through, but not his chest. Pausing for a moment he took a deep breath in, and then let it all out and tried again. And got stuck.

I hefted my rock. 'Another bar?'

He pulled himself back, swearing roundly. We set to work at another bar, Rodden muttering to himself, scraping his knuckles, swearing, and then pounding even harder.

'There's no use rushing,' I told him. 'You'll only make a hash of it.'

'I am sick of being in this cage,' he snapped. The bar came loose, but could not be pulled free. 'Stand back, I'm trying again.'

The half an inch wriggle room we'd created seemed to make a difference. Rodden got further this time, and with a strangled, drawn out groan he slowly, agonisingly, wrenched himself through. With a victorious shout he hurled the rock he was holding against the far wall. There was a crack, and a great cascade of stones fell.

After several anguished moments of silence while we looked at the rocks around us, wondering if they would all come crashing onto our heads, I said, 'What an irony if the whole place had caved in then. Come on. Let's see if we really can get out of here.'

He caught my sleeve as I turned. 'Wait. Before we leave, do you forgive me?'

Startled, I stared up at him. There was an intense look in his eyes.

'You're angry with me. I have to know if you forgive me.'

I pulled free of his grasp. There was another distant rumble, and the rocks beneath us shook. 'We haven't got time for this. Besides, you haven't even said you're sorry.'

CHAPTER THIRTEEN

King Askar's face was expressionless and there was an uneasy silence in the great hall. Queen Ulah sat beside him on their thrones in the palace at Xallantaria, and the court surrounded us, dozens of men and women decked out in their finery.

'So you see,' I said, finishing my story, 'I fear for the safety of the city.' I hadn't told them Garrick had been my father. I hadn't told them that he'd wanted to make me queen of Lharmell. But I had told them the dying king's words, and the very real threat all the surviving Lharmellins and harmings posed to Pergamia. Lharmell was falling apart. They needed a new home, and Pergamia was the closest country to Lharmell.

Looking closer at the queen I saw there were lines and sleeplessness etched into her soft face. The pretty, pleasant woman I had known was almost unrecognisable. But she at least was attending to me. The king was more than expressionless; his eyes were vacant and I was sure he hadn't attended to my words.

I turned to the queen. 'Your majesty, we should prepare for an attack from Lharmell.'

A rumble of consternation rolled around the room, and I was glad. They should be worried. Beside me I could feel Rodden wound as tight as a coil. We'd had to dig ourselves out of Garrick's underground chambers in places. We were filthy and ragged, hands raw with the effort. No time had been wasted in presenting ourselves to the king and queen, stealing two brants and flying them south to Pergamia. We'd been careful to put them down on the beach and walk the rest of the way to the palace, lest we be mistaken for the enemy and shot down. The two birds, untethered, flew by instinct back to Lharmell.

The king started to laugh. Softly at first, shoulders shaking. Then he put a hand up to his face, sniggers erupting behind it.

'My dear,' the queen cried in dismay. She put out her hands as if to comfort a distressed person, not one who was overtaken with mirth. The court fell silent, watching him. Rodden shot me a troubled look.

'What's wrong with him?' I hissed under my breath. All around me, courtiers looked embarrassed, and their gazes rested on anything but the king.

Queen Ulah stood and announced, 'The king is unwell.' Attendants came and led the king away, the queen following. As one, the court bowed them out of the room. The king's shoulders were still shaking as he left.

'What was he laughing at?' I asked Rodden. 'I know we look a fright, but is it funny?'

Rodden was looking at the courtier's faces. They were embarrassed, not surprised. 'I don't think he was laughing at us.'

'Zeraphina!' Someone was pushing through the clusters of people. Prince Amis, my sister's husband and King Askar's son. He was a tall, fair man with a sweet, handsome face. A face that was etched with worry like his mother's had been. He reached us and took both of my hands in his. 'Thank the stars you are safe. And you Rodden. I've been so worried these past weeks.'

I tried to take my hands back, protesting that I was filthy.

'Never mind that now. You spoke of danger to the city. What has happened?'

'We will tell you, but is your father unwell?'

'My father –' He was conscious of the courtiers listening. 'Come, I will tell you,' he murmured.

We followed the prince out of the throne room and to a private chamber. Amis ordered basins of warm water for us, and clean robes. Two attendants brought basins and towels, and set up a screen in the corner of the room.

'Please, you must want to wash and make yourselves more comfortable.'

'What I want is for someone to heed what we have to say,' I said. 'The palace is in great danger.'

'The soldiers are atop the battlements. They will warn us if we're attacked.'

It was true, I had seen the archers atop the walls, and their arrows had yelbar tips. Amis motioned me to the screen. I did badly want to wash, and I hadn't seen a towel so soft and white in a very long time.

'All right. But you must talk while we wash,' Rodden said, turning to a basin on the table and began unfastening his gauntlets. I stepped behind the screen and stripped to the waist. There was a washcloth next to the basin on a little stand and I used it to sponge myself down. The water quickly turned a dirty pink from all the dried blood and dust that coated me. The abrasions on my hands stung as I washed.

Amis spoke. 'My father hasn't been himself for several weeks. He had a strange turn, and after he was … different.' Helplessness and confusion made his voice flat. 'There isn't a thing we can do. The physicians have given up on him, telling us his recovery is out of their hands. Mostly he is stern and silent, and while the court thinks this is unusual, they are not alarmed. It is the fits of giggling that we have tried to hide. We are not always able to.'

'And you and your mother?' I called.

He sighed. 'We are well, but we are all so dreadfully worried. There has been no improvement in my father for some time now.'

I took off the rest of my clothes and washed my feet, and then pulled the soft robe that had been laid over the screen around me and tied it at the front. I emerged, and saw Rodden shrugging into his robe.

'I'm so sorry, Amis,' I said.

Amis pulled himself up with a deep breath, as if shaking off his melancholy. 'It is what it is.' He gazed at me, and a frown darkened his features. He reached out a hand to touch a silvery scar on my neck. 'Folsum should pay dearly for what he did.'

Prince Amis had been the only one to defend me when Folsum's sister, Penritha, had denounced me at court. I took his hand in mine and squeezed it, gently pulling it away from my neck. I didn't mind the scars that criss-crossed my back. With all the things I had done it was a wonder I didn't have more.

'Folsum is dead,' I replied.

Amis stared at me in shock. 'By the stars, Zeraphina, what happened?'

Impatient to get back to the more pressing matter, I said, 'I killed him. Not on purpose – not exactly. He was attacking Griffin and I shoved him away, and he fell down some stairs.'

Both Rodden and Amis stared at me. Rodden, as Raufo, had known Folsum was dead, but he didn't know why or how. It would have been strange for Raufo to question me too closely about the prince.

'Shall we go up onto the battlements? I want to know what's happening,' I said to them before they could open their mouths.

'Of course, let me get you some –' but he was interrupted by a trill and the beating of wings, and two dark shapes raced into the room.

'Leap!' A large, silvery creature was butting against my legs. His green eyes looking up at me. I scooped him up and held him tight against me. Over our heads, Griffin was doing circuits of the room. She settled on a chair back and made little noises in the back of her throat. With a gentle finger I reached out and stroked the short, brown feathers at her neck, blinking back tears. 'They're here. How are they here?'

The answer to that stepped through the door. 'Hello, Fina. I am glad you're all right.' Lilith stood hesitating in the doorway, looking very pretty in a pale blue dress, her burnished curls falling over one shoulder. She smiled tentatively but her eyes were worried, as if she wasn't sure how she would be received. I moved to embrace her but remembered I had Leap in my arms. He dug his claws in, enough to cling to me, but not enough to prick.

'Sorry, I know you don't like them,' I said, unable to go to her.

'No, it's all right,' she said, coming forward to kiss me. She gave Leap a pat on the top of his head. 'Ever since you disappeared I've been taking care of them. They can be quite sweet … when they want to be. They've missed you terribly.'

I remembered how, in my stupor, they'd tried to comfort me, but not understood why I wasn't the person I had been. It wasn't any wonder that they'd eventually left my room. I had thought I'd never see them again, that after I disappeared from Amentia they would have gone back into the forest they'd once emerged from and turn wild.

'What if I'd never come back?' I asked Lilith.

Lilith gave a half shrug. 'I'd have looked after them forever.'

My eyes filled again and I buried my face in Leap's fur. I managed to get one arm around Lilith and Leap got squeezed in our embrace, but he didn't seem to mind.

'The battlements?' Amis asked, amused by our face-wiping and hiccupping.

'Yes, please,' I said. I glanced at Rodden. He had withdrawn from the three of us and stood, jaw clenched, with his hands behind his back and eyes averted. When Leap jumped down to wind between his legs in greeting, he didn't move.

'Fina, I'll find you some clothes,' Lilith offered. 'Amis will do the same for Rodden.'

'Are you coming?' I asked Rodden from the doorway.

After a long moment he gave a short nod, and followed.

The sky was dark despite it being only a few hours past midday, and there was a heavy, acrimonious scent in the air. Dozens of guards were posted atop the crenelated walls, all with bows at the ready and wearing grim faces.

Soft flakes were falling sparsely from the sky, and the woods that ran down to the northern coast were frosted with white. But it wasn't snow. I ran my finger over a stone, and the flakes crumbled into dust. It was ash. The northern horizon was obscured with thick grey-white clouds that seemed to rise from the ground rather than descend from the air, and then spread out across the sky. Clouds that rained ash. I had never seen or heard of the like.

'What is it?' I asked, turning to Rodden.

Rodden looked graver than ever. 'Do you remember me telling that Lharmell is little more than a giant, spent volcano? The basin in the circle of the tors is what remains of the crater. It seems like the earthquakes that destroyed the tor-line have woken the volcano.'

'It's erupted?' I asked.

'Not yet. We would have felt it. It's only smoking at the moment.'

Yet.

Amis looked at Rodden and me. 'This is good, isn't it? This must mean it's ended.'

I chewed my lip. Rodden said nothing. 'My – someone, a harming, gave me a warning before he died. He said even though I had broken the tor-lines, we hadn't won.' I bit off before saying *my father* as Lilith didn't know about Garrick. She'd stayed inside the castle, not wanting to come up to the battlements. I had to tell her before Amis knew.

Leap and Griffin were with me though, staying close to my side now we'd been reunited. Griffin sat atop the battlements, wings hunched. She stared out across the narrow sea as if she could see all the way to Lharmell. Every now and then she'd ruffle her feathers and dislodge a dusting of small grey flakes. Leap sat at my feet. I was shod now in soft-soled boots, and Leap's head butted against my calf. I leaned down and gave him a pat.

'Can anything survive on Lharmell now?' Amis asked. 'Rodden, you've been very quiet.'

Rodden cleared his throat. 'Zeraphina and I got out. Others could too. We've underestimated the scale of Lharmell before. Its underground tracts …' He looked at me. 'Did any Lharmellins survive the rock fall?'

'Some of them, I think, but it was so dark and confusing down there.'

'Can you live so close to a smoking volcano?' Amis asked.

'I don't know,' I replied. 'There's so much we don't know. I don't have a good feeling, though I can't trust that feeling because I'm … hazy still.' I looked away, ashamed of the reasons for my lack of clarity.

'No,' Rodden interrupted. 'You're right. I feel it too. Like a huge, angry swarm of bees just over the horizon.'

'Yes, exactly,' I said. In that moment I wanted to grasp his hand in gratitude. But I didn't.

'Y' highnesses.' A deep voice interrupted us. It was Hoggit, the captain of the guard. The man was tall and robust, with a weathered and pocked face. He held a tiny scroll, the sort you might attach to the leg of a homing pigeon, made tinier by his large hands.

'Hoggit,' Amis said, incredulous. 'Delivering messages? Are all the runners a-bed?'

'The boy brought it to me, and I had to bring it straight to you myself – and the princess here. I heard she was back. Very glad to see you well, princess.'

'Thank you, Hoggit. And I you.'

The smile faded from Amis's face and he took the message from Hoggit. 'It is for both of us?' He read the scroll, and his face went slack with shock.

'What is it?' I asked.

Rodden took the message from Amis and read it. 'It is from your mother. They are under attack.'

'Harmings?' I asked, because my head was filled with Lharmell.

'No. It is Ansengaad.'

Chapter Fourteen

'We must send soldiers at once,' Lilith said, pacing up and down her bedchamber.

'We have sent men,' Amis said. He was standing by the table, trying to guide her into a chair. But she would not sit. 'You mother understands –'

'I have seen no men,' she snapped, wheeling to face him. 'Where are these men you speak of?'

'Your highness, it would take many weeks for Pergamian soldiers to reach Amentia,' Rodden said. He stood by the cold fireplace, hands clasped behind his back. Ever since the message arrived he had looked graver and graver. 'There are the Pergamian men garrisoned in Fort Skarn, not two days' ride from the Amentine capital. The king of Scarnkan is our ally; he will send his own soldiers with them.'

Two bright spots burned on Lilith's cheeks. She looked between Amis and Rodden. 'But we have sent none of our Xallentarian men to aid my mother. She is under *attack*.'

'By the time any men barracked here would reach her it may be too –' Amis stopped, seeing Lillith's horrified face. He finished, 'We are doing all we can. Without the men at Scarn we would have been able to do nothing.'

'What is Ansengaad doing?' I muttered. I was sitting on my hands on the chest at the foot of the bed. 'They could hold the castle, but they will start a war with Pergamia. Pergamia is far mightier than Ansengaad, and its troops will march if they must.' I looked to Amis for confirmation, and he nodded. The Pergamian husband of an Amentine princess wouldn't let such an affront go unpunished.

'Hold the castle? You think they have already taken it, then?' Rodden asked.

'No, they can't have,' Lilith protested.

'Sister, you were there that day. Folsum's men were *inside* the castle when he died.'

'No, see, mother was too clever.' Lilith's eyes were wide with excitement as she told us. 'We discovered Folsum's body before his soldiers did, and hid it. You remember that both his soldiers and ours were unarmed as a show of good faith? Mother knew where their weapons were stored. She wasn't supposed to, of course, but you know how shrewd she is. She gave secret orders that their weapons be hid, and then –'

'Oh, stars, she didn't murder them all, did she?' I exclaimed.

'Of course not. They were given a lot of unwatered wine to drink to celebrate your impending nuptials, and when they were thoroughly drunk, our soldiers herded them out of the castle and barred the gates behind them.'

Amis bit back a smile. Even Rodden's mouth twitched.

'And they didn't force their way back in?' I asked.

'How could they? They had no weapons. We gave them the prince's body, and they all went home.' There was silence as we let this sink in. Then I covered my face and groaned into my hands.

'What are you moaning about, Zeraphina?' Lilith snapped, anger creeping into her voice again. 'It was to right your silly mess that we had to act so.'

'That is why I am groaning. I am picturing Princess Penritha's face when she witnesses the return of her humiliated, weaponless soldiers bearing the body of her dead brother.'

'She wants revenge,' Rodden said.

'Precisely. And she doesn't care if she starts a war with Amentia.'

'Why should she start a war with Amentia? It was you who pushed him down the stairs,' Lilith pointed out. 'Best thing for him,' she muttered.

'Yes, but who gave the soldiers wine and then presented them with their dead prince's body?'

'Oh. Yes, I see.' Lilith gnawed on her lip.

There was never going to be a good time to tell her about our father, but now seemed as good a time as any. I was just as worried as she was but Amis had already done what could be done for our mother for the moment. It wasn't wise for him to send soldiers away to Amentia now for reasons other than the ones he had voiced. They might be sorely needed here very soon. Lilith had a right to know why.

'Lilith, there's something I need to talk to you about.'

Rodden gave me a sharp look. Then he looked at Amis. 'Let's talk further on this elsewhere.'

I was grateful for his tact, but Lilith wasn't having any of it.

'No, we talk here and we figure this out together. It's up to us, what with your father –' She broke off, seeing Amis's stricken face. 'My love, I didn't mean it,' she said, going to him. 'The king will recover soon.'

Amis didn't look like he agreed, but he forced a smile to show he wasn't angry.

'What do you have to tell me?' Lilith asked me.

I was at a loss as to where to start. Several moments passed before Rodden took a breath and said, 'While I was in Lharmell several months ago, orders, if you can call them that, were circulating that Zeraphina was to be brought back at all costs. Not to be killed, but to be crowned. I never knew who that person was, but I thought that if …' He broke off and looked away. 'But never mind that part. I found Zeraphina, we came to Lharmell, and she discovered who that person was.'

Lilith looked at me.

'He was very different, and I barely recognised him,' I said. 'We only had that one painting after all. But it was him.'

'Who?'

'Our father, King Garrick.' Lilith looked dumb-founded so I hurried on. 'He didn't die. Mother only told us he did because that was her best guess in the circumstances.'

'He's alive?'

Drat. I could have slapped myself for not leading with that. 'No. No, he's dead now. He died yesterday.'

'My father who I though was dead is now dead. Again. Yesterday,' Lilith repeated. And then she burst into tears.

Amis led Lilith to a chair and kissed the top of her head. He shot me a look that said, *Will you be all right?* I nodded, and he and Rodden quietly departed. I shooed Leap and Griffin after them. Lilith might have a new-found tolerance for them, but I didn't want to stretch my luck.

As soon as the door closed Lilith unleashed a loud sob. I sat beside her, patting her sleeve. Lilith knew I wasn't good with sobbing, so she did it into her arms.

'I'm sorry,' she quavered, sitting up. 'It's all been so much. You and Rodden turning up suddenly, and poor mother under attack. And now father. He was really alive all that time? And he never told us?'

'He was a harming,' I said.

'But he was still our father. Why didn't he tell us?'

I shook her arm gently. 'No, he wasn't. That wasn't our father. I thought it was too, at first, but he was only a harming that lived in his body and had his memories. He didn't treat me like a father treats a daughter, and he would have done the same thing to you if he'd had the chance.'

Lilith wiped her eyes and studied my face. 'Done what?'

'He wanted to make me queen of Lharmell against my will. I told him I didn't want that but he said it didn't matter what I wanted. We were prisoners. He kept Rodden in a cell.'

'How awful of him.'

I considered this. 'Well, Rodden did try to murder him. And I stupidly stopped him – I regret that now. But I wasn't to know then. I had only just found out who he was. I thought that maybe …' There hadn't been much time to think when I'd seen Rodden approaching Garrick with a yelbar knife.

'How did he die?'

'You've seen that the air is full of ash, and felt the earthquakes these past months?' She nodded. 'The tor-line, a sort of connecting force between Lharmell and all the harmings in the world, has been pulling the mountains apart. Not fast enough for me, though. I thought that if I could break the tor-lines then I could destroy what made Lharmell powerful. I only had a few days before Garrick was going to force me to become a harming, and Rodden, too. I found a way to harness the power of the tor-lines and it caused a massive earthquake. We were deep underground, and there was a lot of falling rock …'

Lilith nodded and gripped my hands in hers. 'Thank the stars you and Rodden made it out alive.'

'We nearly didn't.'

Lilith's eyes filled with tears again as she looked at the cuts on my hands. 'Oh, Fina. I've been such a rotten sister.'

I smiled. 'No more rotten than me. I'm thoroughly ashamed of my behaviour since I thought Rodden died, and before then, too. I acted very spoiled and selfish.'

'You were doing important work with Rodden,' Lilith pointed out.

'But I needn't have been such an ass about it. I snuck away from the palace twice with Rodden when you'd told me not to.'

'It wasn't my place to tell you no. I was pre-occupied with what the court would think of me because of you.'

'And then I left you with Folsum's dead body to explain to the Ansengaad soldiers.'

Lilith shushed me with a small gesture. 'All that has been unavoidable. You might have always been my wilful little sister, but you have never betrayed me before the court as I did you when Princess Penritha came to take you back to Ansengaad. I have no excuse except that I was angry, but that is no excuse at all. Amis was the only one who stood up for you, and it should have been both of us. I'm thoroughly ashamed of myself.'

'Lilith, dear, you needn't be.'

'But I am. Do you forgive me?'

I realised I'd stopped being angry with Lilith a long time ago. She'd been put in an impossible position between myself and mother, not to mention the pressure put on her as Amis's new wife. 'Of course, sister. And do you forgive me?'

'There is nothing to forgive.' Lilith's top lip wobbled once more, but she said, 'What about Rodden?'

I felt my face go hard. 'What about him?'

'Do you forgive him for whatever has happened? Fina, what *has* happened? He was dead, wasn't he?'

'I don't want to talk about it.'

'You were so wretched when you thought he was dead. I thought you'd be overjoyed to find it not so.'

So had I, all those nights I'd looked at the cold, Brivoran sky and wished everything I loved away for him not to be dead. But some wishes come with too high a price.

Lilith reached out to touch my hand. 'I know something terrible must have happened between the two of you since you left here all those months ago. But I also know how strong your friendship was. I thought perhaps that you even –' She broke off, frowning, and her head turned toward the door. She was listening. 'How strange. Why are the bells ringing?'

Now that she'd drawn my attention to it I heard it too, a cacophony of urgent sound. They were the bells that usually rang for celebrations, but there was nothing merry in their peals now. 'It is an alarm. I think we must be under attack.'

I found Rodden and Amis by the armoury, buckling on gauntlets and shrugging into armour. The prince was being helped into heavy plate. Rodden wore quilted leather armour. It wasn't as robust, but it was much lighter. Rodden would sacrifice some protection to be able to remain nimble.

The armoury was in the heart of the castle, a great, fortified room that held the bulk of the palaces defences, what wasn't held in the barracks. The palace guards had formed a chain and were handing swords, bows and arrows out of the fortified room. Runners took armloads away in every direction.

'Lharmell or Ansengaad?' I asked Rodden and Amis.

'Lharmell,' Rodden replied. 'Where are you going?' he asked when I turned away.

I had been about to go to Lilith's room and find something suitable to fire arrows in. The dress I wore was too tight about the shoulders. 'Nowhere,' I replied quickly. If he told me to take cover in the cellars with Lilith and the other women I would slap him.

'Then put these on and get a weapon, and be quick about it.' He thrust a uniform at me.

I turned to run to Lilith's room to change, but then looked back at Amis. 'Has the king been informed?' He'd be able to hear the bells. I wondered if, in his confusion, he understood what they meant. I thought of his wise, friendly face as I had known it, with the intelligent sparkle in his eyes. There'd been none of that sparkle in court earlier. The thought of those eyes now filled with confusion and fear at the sound of the pealing bells made something inside me twist painfully.

'He has been told,' was all Amis said, and I knew from his tone that there was little chance the king had understood the message. There was a tightness to Amis's mouth, and apprehension in his eyes. It was little wonder. The first time the palace was under attack in a century or more and the king was not fit to lead the defence. Amis was a capable young man, but I could see he felt unprepared for this.

'We always knew this day would come,' Rodden said to Amis, sensing his friend's anxiety. 'The palace is prepared and well defended. It won't be an easy battle for them.'

'And for us?' Amis muttered under his breath.

CHAPTER FIFTEEN

In any normal siege, the defenders sit atop their high walls and hurl missiles at siege engines and pour hot oil down on their enemies' heads. The danger is spread beneath you and surges up on ladders or batters through doors. But when you're defending a palace from Lharmell, the attack comes from the air.

I had changed in Lilith's room and pulled on a pair of her riding boots. The leather armour Rodden had given me was for a man and too large and bulky, and after several attempts to winch it tighter against my body with a pair of Lilith's belts, I cast it aside. The only protection I wore were wrist guards, but I was an archer. If a Lharmellin or harming got close enough to run me through I couldn't wield a sword to defend myself in any case.

The corridors were empty as I ran to the northern wall. The bells had ceased ringing, and the only sound was a faint murmuring. The sound, punctuated by thin shrieks, grew louder as I ran up the spiral staircase to the ramparts and burst out into the fresh air. It was afternoon, but the light was strange. In the west, several hours from setting, the sun hung like a giant red eye above the city.

The battle was raging all around me. Brants were screaming and wheeling overhead, bearing harming riders who slashed at the soldiers. Pressed back against the walls was a line of archers, giving space to the soldiers who stood protectively before them. To my left and right I could see messy knots of figures fighting hand-to-hand where harmings must have dropped from their mounts.

'*Draw.*' That was Captain Hoggit's voice. I couldn't see him past a turn in the wall but I recognised his voice. The order was repeated along the battlements, fading from my ears. On the horizon, darks specks studded the sky, growing larger. Another wave of harmings were coming, and I still didn't have a weapon.

A hand clamped on my arm, and I turned. It was Rodden, and he clasped two bows. 'Come with me.'

We threaded our way through the men, crouching low. I could see little in this sea of bow butts and booted feet, but heard Amis's shout to the soldiers to reform their line. The archers were poised and silent. The soldiers before them beat their swords against their shields and roared.

We came to the northern turret, Rodden opened the door, and we ran up the spiral staircase. Every turn in the stair we had to step around an archer standing at an arrow slit, his bow drawn and arrow trained on the north.

Rodden's room had barely altered since I'd last been in it. Books and scrolls covered every flat surface, and the narrow bed lay unmade. Up in the rafters something fluttered. A bat, I supposed. A larger shaped moved, and the white dish of an owl's face looked down at me.

Rodden went to the window in the northern wall and flung back the shutters. We watched the approaching figures in the sky as we laid out the quiver of arrows Rodden carried and tested our bows.

'Why do they make such a din?' I asked, referring to the noise the soldiers were making.

In answer Rodden leaned out the window and peered to the west, squinting into the red sun. 'To draw the enemy here, and not to the city.'

'Is it not guarded?'

'It is, but it is not as well defended as the castle. And the citizens don't shelter behind stone walls, but tiled cottages.'

I leaned out the window, too. The city was shrouded with drifting smoke, but from what I could see the city looked as much as it always did, with its short spires, terracotta roofs and stout city walls. Nothing was aflame or amiss. But the flecks on the horizon were recognisable as brants, now, and many were headed for the city as well as the palace.

There were both plain and yelbar arrows laid before us on the sill. We chose plain arrows now, and drew our bows. When the cry came to loose, our arrows joined to scores of others fleeting through the air towards the giant birds and riders. Several birds faltered mid-air, and others screamed and fell, taking their riders with them. Most climbed sharply and kept coming.

We had our bows drawn again when the brants hurtled over the battlements. Some riders dropped atop the walls, harmings brandishing swords. They launched themselves on the soldiers. Other harmings dropped into the bailey. I heard rather than saw the clash of fighting there.

One brant whistled past the northern turret and we both loosed our arrows. Rodden's passed through the bird's tail feathers. Mine stuck in the harming's leg, and it merely yanked the point out and passed over the wall toward the bailey. I cursed and fitted a yelbar arrow into my bow instead. After twenty minutes I'd picked off three harmings, two from brant-back and one atop the battlements. Rodden had felled two brants and riders. There was another wave of brants on the horizon, fast approaching. We could hear clashes and screams from the bailey.

This was what my father had meant when he'd said it wasn't over. He'd never dared attack Pergamia in his lifetime, but Lharmell was desperate now. They had to find another place to call home before the island tore itself apart. The desperation worried me. I could see the harmings fighting with everything they had.

Rodden looked over his shoulder at the shuttered southern window. 'Do you want to pick off the riders, or shoot the harmings in the bailey?'

'The riders.' I wanted to see the horizon and know how many were coming. I realised that if I shot a harming out of the saddle, or once he or she had dropped of its own volition onto the ramparts or into the bailey, the brant that had carried it banked in a tight circle and returned to Lharmell. To collect another harming, I presumed. But if I aimed for the brant instead and missed, then another harming would breach the palace walls. And mostly I missed when I aimed at the birds, large as they were. They flew swiftly and evasively and were difficult targets.

In the end I didn't resolve on either target, but simply loaded my bow with yelbar tips and took my shots where and when I could. All the while I wondered, Where are the Lharmellins? They were deadly and fearsome and could command strange powers. They could draw sudden storms. Acid rain. And merely frighten the troops with their appearance.

Just as the sun was setting and the murky light was fading from the sky, the brants stopped coming. Arms aching, I laid down my bow and crossed the room to the window where Rodden stood. He had his right shoulder in his left hand and was rubbing it absently. Torches were being lit all around the bailey below, and they revealed the destruction of the battle. Soldiers' bodies were being laid in neat rows on the hard packed earth. Dead harmings were being loaded into a cart.

'What will happen to them?' I asked, referring to all the dead bodies. I was thinking about Renata, and what she might be doing at this very moment. Perhaps she too was watching the aftermath of a battle from the top of her castle walls. There was a lot of blood, and it showed as dark black streaks on the ground.

'The soldiers' bodies will be given back to their families,' Rodden replied. 'The harmings will be buried in pits somewhere outside the city.'

'There are no prisoners,' I noticed.

'The harmings never surrendered. The last one alive knew he was the last one, but he didn't lay down his weapon.'

'Do you think that was really the last one?'

He gave me a long look, and then his eyes went to the window in the northern wall of the turret. 'No. Just the last one today. There are more in Lharmell. And there are Lharmellins. And now they're desperate.'

We followed the trail of weary soldiers into the great hall. Formerly a bright and merry place, there was a sombre mood beneath that roof now. The thrones atop the dais were empty. Most of the courtiers were absent, too, except the few who had taken up arms and fought.

Perhaps to distract the soldiers from the king's absence, Prince Amis roamed among the long tables, stopping to talk every few feet. I watched him, and his expression was calm, almost genial. But his hands gave away his true feelings. His knuckles were white where they rested atop his sword hilt.

Rodden and I collected a bowl of stew and found places at a bench. For a while we listened to the conversations around us. Soldiers were recounting the battle and the part they had played. The strangeness of the enemy. Every now and then one of them would glance at the throne where the king should sit, and then back at his food.

'Where do you think King Askar is?' I asked Rodden in a low voice.

'In his bed, perhaps. He must be in quite a state for Amis and the queen to keep him away at time like this.'

I wondered where Lilith was. Still in the cellars, or back in the solar with the other women, I supposed. Like me, she wouldn't know what to worry about first: another attack from Lharmell, or our mother under siege in Amentia.

'How many miles is it from Fort Skarn to Prestoral?' I asked.

Rodden looked at me like he hadn't the slightest idea what I was talking about. Then he sighed, remembering, and rubbed a hand over his hair. 'Sixty, seventy miles.'

The terrain around my home was mountainous. Quite strenuous for a horse, let alone one carrying an armoured man and his weapons. 'Amis said two days' ride. But with hills and valleys it might take three days, or even four.'

'A siege is a long affair.'

'That's not very comforting,' I snapped.

Rodden scowled down into his food. Ordinarily he would snap back if I talked to him like that, both of us knowing that neither of us meant our barbs to stick. But things had changed, and perhaps I did mean to wound.

'Would you like to see her?' he asked after a long moment.

'What does that mean?' And then realisation dawned. 'You could see her. You could travel there out of your body.'

'I could take you, too, I think.'

'What? How?'

'I'm not certain I could, but I have read that it is possible. And it would only be for a very short while as it is very tiring.'

I didn't feel I had the right to ask him, not when we had fought so long and hard all afternoon and would doubtlessly have to do the same upon the morrow. Asking a friend to exhaust himself was one thing. But someone I didn't know how I felt about was another. I would be beholden to him, and I didn't want that.

'We shouldn't, then. You need your strength.' I turned back to my dinner, forcing my face to remain neutral.

'I am going anyway. We may as well try to go together.'

My spoon dredged up a piece of carrot from the bottom of the bowl. I shook my head.

'Very well,' he replied, and his voice was tight and unfamiliar. He stood and walked away.

I watched his retreating back, wondering why I felt bereft when it was what I had wanted. I was too sick at heart to eat. Too tired to sleep. So I followed him. He went to his turret, of course. There were dozens of men atop the parapets and torches blazed in the bailey. The night was a cold one, for Pergamia. On the breeze I thought I heard snatches of Lharmellin song. But I wasn't thinking about Lharmell right now. I climbed the stairs to the turret room.

He was in the centre of the room, a candle burning on the table. Both hands were braced on his desk, and he looked up when he saw me enter.

'Since when do you give up so easily?' I asked.

He sat down in the high-backed chair and regarded me. 'I'm not fighting with you.'

'Yes, you are,' I corrected. We had to fight. Otherwise there would be nothing, and I couldn't bear it.

'What is the point?' he asked.

'Fighting is better than silence.'

'I didn't offer you silence. I offered to ease your mind about your mother, and you turned it down. You don't want anything from me *but* to fight.'

I gave a strangled cry and put my fists to my head. There was so much anger inside of me and I couldn't disentangle what was anger towards him, anger towards myself and sheer worry over everything that was happening. 'That's never stopped you before.'

'Things are different now.' He was so calm, sitting there with his hands folded over his chest and his hard, narrowed eyes boring into me. The eyes betrayed his true feelings. He was not as sanguine as he pretended to be. 'Do you know why you're so angry, Zeraphina?'

I threw up my hands. 'Oh, please, tell me.'

'You want to forgive me, but you're too proud.'

I stared at him. 'Go on. Finish that thought.'

His mouth twitched. 'I don't know what you mean.'

'Yes you do.'

A long moment passed. His eyes were just as hard as they had been, but there was veiled mirth in the set of his mouth. Finally he said, 'You're too proud, *princess.*'

I let out a scream and flew around the table at him. He was up in a flash to grab at my wrists before they could land any blows, but he wasn't quite quick enough. I punched his chest and shoulders, and all the while he was laughing, and, between laughs, speaking, but I wasn't listening.

I yanked my hand from his grasp and punched him in the stomach. That drew a satisfying *oof* from him. There was a booted foot next to mine and I stomped on it, hard. Pain flashed through his eyes. Then something else flashed through them. I went for the foot again and he launched himself at me with an 'Oh, no you don't.' We landed on the floor in a tangle, and suddenly his lips was on mine. His mouth was hot and his hands were in my hair, not holding my wrists, and his body lay pressed tightly against me. Suddenly I forgot that I wanted to beat him to the consistency of a squashed melon. The world contracted to the space of a few square feet. It was particularly vivid in the places where my hands gripped the sides of his back. He'd taken off the leather armour and wore only a rough shirt. I could feel the results of all the months he'd spent being Raufo and wielding a heavy axe. As he kissed me, curiosity made my hands explore further afield, up to his shoulders and then down to his hips. Curiosity, and appreciation. I was just wondering whether the skin at his lower back would be soft and smooth, and tugging on his shirt to find out, when he stopped kissing me and said, 'I don't think you'd forgive me even if I begged for it.'

I pushed him away and sat up. My hair was in a snarl and my lips tingled. I swiped the back of my hand across my mouth. 'I'd forgive you if you deserved it.'

He stood up and went back to the high-backed chair. There didn't seem to be anything for him to laugh at now. 'Why won't you let me do this thing for you? Don't you want to know what's happening in Amentia?'

'Of course I do, you ass.'

'Well then?' His gaze was goading and his chest was lifting with heavy breaths.

My mind kept wanting to dwell on the sensations my lips and body were sending it. Why was I being so stubborn again? I couldn't remember. If he didn't care about being too exhausted to fight tomorrow, then neither did I. 'Fine. Let's do it then. But it doesn't mean I forgive you.'

The problem was I didn't know how we were going to travel outside our bodies together, and neither did Rodden. He came around the desk again and put his hands on my shoulders. I shrugged him off. 'No, you don't.'

'I'm not going to kiss you,' he said, exasperated. He put his hands back and frowned as if he was thinking. Seconds passed.

'I don't feel anything.'

'Would you be quiet?'

'Fine.'

'That's not being quiet.'

'*Fine*,' I grated through clenched teeth.

Rodden closed his eyes. Impatient, and not very hopeful, my eyes wandered the room. If he tidied up the place could be quite cosy. Roll up some of the scrolls, for starters, and put away all the dirty glass jars he did experiments in.

There was a tug where his hands held my shoulders. 'Stop pulling at me, will you?'

But he wasn't moving, and his face beneath his burn had gone very pale and slack. I felt like I was being dragged underwater by a deep ocean current, and panicked.

'No. Wait, I'm not ready.' I tried to fight him but the water closed over my head and I was pulled under, unable to breathe.

Chapter Sixteen

There was nothing out there. Not a sound. Not a bird, not a breeze. There were no lights to see in the sky. No sky. Not even any up, because there up or down were both the same, and the reverse.

I was alone, suspended like a drop of water on the end of a leaf. Only the leaf wasn't real because leaves and water drops needed things like trees and *down*.

'Why don't I just let go?'

'Who said that?' I said, trembling in fear. 'Don't let go. I'll fall.' I shook, and there was laughter, the only sound in the black void.

'I won't fall,' said the other voice.

'I am glad for you! But I might fall.'

'No, I won't.'

'What?'

More laughter, and more shaking. But it wasn't fear making me shake. 'I'm laughing,' I said in surprise.

'Well of course I am. It's funny.'

'Where are you?' I said.

'I'm right here. Let go.'

I let go, and laughed some more.

'I should open my eyes,' I said into the void, because there was only one voice, and that voice was mine. But I wasn't alone.

I opened them. There was light in the world, a billion pinpricks of diamond light. Stretching luxuriously, I turned over and over, seeing the world flash bright, dark, and bright again. I was seeing everything for the first time, and just as it had always been.

'I'm a *we*. It's us. How lovely to be us. And we know the way.' Amentia was that way, the direction that would be south and a little to the west if we were in our earthly bodies. But south and west were no more directions here than the colour green was. We flew for miles, part of the wind itself, gliding and dipping on currents of air. If I'd had eyes to shed tears I would have, feeling the freedom of it all.

'Why must we feel so angry all the time? Why must you?'

'We are a *we*,' came the rejoinder, and the two halves burrowed closer together. There was a great deal of fear. There was also regret. Images flashed into our mind. Of Lharmell. Of the places that meant home. One home was a strong picture of almost smothering security, a mountain castle with a stubborn queen. It was under threat, and that was a reminder of its preciousness. The other home was a mere sketch, grey and watery in both appearance and memory. The papery weight of books and smoking jars. And loneliness. Only some bright and golden recollections relieved its isolation. A spitting-cat of a girl, hauled out from under the bed. The girl, now a little older and unkempt, skin browned in the sun and travel-weary, curled up in a chair read aloud from a book. The memories both delighted and saddened us. Other memories, more recent, swam into view. The same girl was grown thin and dull-eyed. She was distant and unpredictable, and little of her former self seemed to remain.

The shock of seeing the difference in this person made the flying thing shudder mid-air, and it coalesced momentarily into two halves.

'I'm sorry,' said the half that wasn't shocked, as if it had wanted to keep that memory to itself. It had seen that girl many times. The halves shuddered back together.

The air currents had brought them all the way to the castle, that *home* place. It was grey and solid in the moonlight, yellow lamplight leaking out into the night. We flew in and out the windows, searching. Scudding over the ground we passed through the smoke and sparks of campfires. In one high window we darted, and a red-headed woman looked up as if struck by a draught.

Then we were leaving, the castle growing smaller and smaller, disappearing among the diamond lights of the heavens.

Breath flooded in. My body was a too-large thing and the world spun round it like toy top wobbling its last. There was a familiar rising sensation in my stomach and I scrambled up and made for the window. I wished I hadn't eaten any beef stew.

Rodden stood behind me, silently rubbing circles on my back as I heaved.

'It doesn't make you sick?' I asked, voice thick, thinking how even stepping onto a boat would make him throw up.

'No, never.'

'She's alive,' I whispered when I was finished. 'Ansengaad hasn't taken the castle yet, but they are camped outside.' I pulled my head in and wiped my mouth on my shirtsleeve. 'Rodden, I –'

'Shh, not now. It's late.' He put me in his narrow bed and gave me a cup of water to drink. Leap and Griffin had found us, and my cat curled into the hollow above my knees. For a while I listened to his purr against my belly, and Rodden move quietly around the room, my eyes closed. The little bed was very comfortable and smelled familiar. The dizziness subsided, and I slept.

CHAPTER SEVENTEEN

It happened very early in the morning. The dawn light was thin through the shroud of smoke and ash, but it wasn't the light that woke us. There was something like a rumbling, heard between waking and sleep. It was the shaking that woke me. Rodden lay beside me on the floor atop a cloak, and he was sitting up, hair at odd angles and face pale with unsatisfying sleep. The confusion I felt was etched on his face, but realisation dawned as the turret began to sway.

I was up by the time he grabbed my hand. Griffin flew straight out the window and Leap bounded for the door. We ran after him, and followed his silvery tail as fast as we could down the spiral stairs. It disappeared after a few turns as we stumbled and lost our footing. There was an awful sound, a low booming, and the crunch of stones.

We made it out onto the parapet and the tower collapsed. A ripple like an ocean wave passed through it, travelling upwards to the blue conical roof, and then it split open like fruit and fell away. Dust flew into the air. What had been solid stone, and home for Rodden for many years, collapsed in a crash in a matter of seconds and was gone.

The quaking ceased. I realised I had one arm wrapped around Rodden and another gripping a crennelation. We went to the wall and looked down. There wasn't much to see but a cloud of dust and a pile of rocks in the shape of something that only vaguely resembled a turret.

'All your things are gone,' I cried. 'All your books and maps. Everything about Lharmell you so patiently studied and assembled for all these years.'

He gazed at the rubble a little longer and then straightened. He looked at me. 'It doesn't seem to move me much. I think I learned all I could learn from my little library.'

'But it was your home.'

He looked a little crestfallen at that. 'I shall make another. The remarkable thing is that we made it out alive.' He made a halting movement of his arm. I sensed that he had been about to put his arm around me and kiss the top of my head, but had checked himself.

I had *sensed* it. Could my mind was finally clearing? Last night I had felt … so many things. Feeling a little bereft, I stooped and gathered Leap into my arms. He was stiff with fright and his eyes very full and dark as he looked about him.

The morning was very grey and still. Soldiers were coming out into the bailey below, staring about them.

It was impossible to tell how early or late it was. The sun was invisible beyond the wan light that filtered through the thick clouds. Everything was dusted with grey ash. Beyond the castle walls the trees were thick with it, and the city was enveloped with white, unseen. Even the battlements were enveloped in places, and we could see only the outlines of guards dotted along the walls.

Rodden looked as if he wished to go downstairs and inside, but something kept him lingering on the battlements. He gazed northwards, though there was nothing to be seen, puzzlement on his brow. I looked, too, expecting to see brants and riders emerging from the swirling clouds. But there was nothing to be seen. 'What is it?'

'It is nothing, I suppose. I can't hear the sea, is all.'

I listened, and nothing reached my ears but the murmurings of the guards.

Rodden shook himself. 'It is the direction of the wind.' He took a last look at the remains of his turret, and then suggested we break our fast in the hall.

The mood was as sombre as it had been the night before. The ladies and lords of the court had emerged, looking pinched and tired. Likely they had spent the night on pallets in the cellars rather than their own bedchamber and had been woken by the quake.

Breakfast was normally a hot savoury pottage but the quake had loosed the stones in the chimneypiece in the kitchens. Day-old bread was handed round instead, and flagons of cold water. Around us, the guards spoke of arrowheads and formations. The families of the court debated whether they should try for their own homes in the countryside.

'Idiots,' Rodden muttered at his piece of bread, as if wondering where to begin with the unappetising chunk. 'They are far safer here than on the road. The king will tell them.'

But the king wouldn't tell them. We both looked to the empty dais. How different the mood in the great hall would have been if King Askar was providing his confident presence. Below the dais Amis stood with a crowd of people around him, attending to them one by one, trying his best to assure and placate. He looked as if he'd slept little. As we watched, two of the king's personal attendants pressed through the crush. They spoke to the prince, and immediately a look of alarm crossed his features and he hurried out.

'Harmings?' I wondered aloud, beginning to stand. But the bells weren't ringing to sound an attack.

'I'm not sure.'

'You go,' I suggested, sitting down again. 'He might need your help, and Amis has had enough people crowding around him without me there as well.'

Rodden put down his untouched bread and hurried out of the hall.

It was surely going to be a long day so I tried to concentrate on eating, tearing off a piece of bread with my teeth and chewing and chewing. It wasn't bad, really, but would be vastly improved by a toasting fork, a fire and some butter. But they weren't to hand. I wondered what else had been destroyed beyond the northern turret and the hearth in the kitchens. There was the city, too, by no means as sturdily built as the palace. How many roofs had been displaced or fires running rampant by the –

Lilith ran into the hall. She stopped in the doorway and stared wildly around. I hurried towards her.

'By the stars, what is the matter? Is it the king?' I asked, seeing her cheeks were wet with tears. Despite her distress she was mindful enough for the need of privacy. She pulled me by the hand out of the hall and behind the door. Her hands shook in mine as she said, 'The king – he's gone down to – Rodden says it's coming in.'

'Where is the king? What's coming in?' I asked, trying to make sense of her near-hysteria.

Lilith swallowed, trying to force calmness enough to speak. 'We didn't realise at first, but the king guessed what would happen. The quake has done something to the ocean, pulled the water far out to sea. Rodden says it will come rushing back, more powerful than any tide.'

Rodden had remarked that he couldn't hear the sea. Something must have been nagging at him then.

'The last thing anyone knows of the king this morning is that he said to the queen he had the power to turn it back,' Lilith said. 'She didn't know what he was talking about, and then he was just gone.'

The bells began to ring, loud and urgent. A cry of alarm rippled round the hall, and then the clash and scrape of wooden benches as everybody rose in unison. The courtiers made for the cellars, thinking it was an attack, but a soldier strode in and bellowed, 'To the battlements. High ground, high ground!'

In the ensuing confusion I was nearly pulled away from Lilith in the crush of people coming out of the hall. I held fast to her hands. 'Rodden and Amis, where are they?'

'They have gone down to the beach to find the king.'

I gave a cry and turned to push my way across the flood of people, trying to get to the front entrance.

'No, Fina, it's not safe.' Lilith grabbed hold of my wrist and held fast with both hands. She was surprisingly strong and I wasn't able to fight my way free of her. There was a yowling at my feet. Leap. He wasn't liking all the trampling feet. With my free hand I hauled him up to my shoulder.

Far off, just discernible over the sound of the bells and the thudding feet, was a roaring sound. It was like a hundred oceans, not one. Lilith's wide eyes met mine. Rodden and Amis were outside, and the tide was coming in.

'Fina, we have get to the battlements,' Lilith said, voice breaking.

We joined the river of people and I looked overhead for Griffin. 'Ouch. Leap, do try not to dig your claws in.' I spied Griffin swooping in and out of an open window, her beak open in a caw that I could not hear over the frightened cries of the courtiers.

Where are they? Can you find them?

She must have heard my entreaty because she immediately took flight in the direction of the coast. Lilith and I followed the courtiers to the battlements. All were urgent, but still we moved painfully slowly. If the palace was swamped with water then surely the battlements were the safest place, but if the harmings chose this moment to attack we would all be vulnerable. The soldiers were armed but the courtiers were not, and there were so many of them that all would be confusion and panic. When we finally emerged into the open air I put Leap atop a wall and whispered to him, 'Go high, and hide.' There were plenty of nooks and crevices where he would be safe. Tail high and straight as a banner he scampered away, safe from stomping feet.

We were waved along the battlements by the soldiers and as we shuffled along I peered down between the crennelations. I could hear the sea, but couldn't see it. Overhead I could see nothing in the sky, but that didn't mean there was nothing there. 'This is terrible. I don't like it at all,' I hissed to Lilith.

'I know, but I couldn't stop them. How foolish to follow the king when they knew what was happening.'

'Yes, Rodden and Amis too, but I meant *this*, being atop the battlements.'

Lilith's eyes shot to the sky. 'Do you think we will be attacked?'

'A mad king absconding and a quake that brings a flood tide, both before breakfast – I would hardly be surprised.'

'Don't *snap* at me, Fina,' protested Lilith.

We were both hissing under our breath lest we be overheard. 'I'm not snapping at you, I'm –'

Griffin's gold shape appeared in the sky and she swooped down to light on the battlements. The image came to me clearly. In her mind's eye I saw nothing but rushing water, a great foamy brown tide advancing at the speed of a horse's gallop. It was beyond the beach and up around the forest line, pushing trees down as it pressed onwards. She'd seen nothing of Rodden and Amis.

A collective cry went up, and Griffin fluttered from the battlements to search further. A rushing sound filled the air and with the soldiers and courtiers we looked down towards the forest. It was as if the ground was a swollen, living thing and was rushing at the walls. The tide wasn't of water, but of debris and mud and broken trees. The wave crashed against the castle walls and began to rise.

I gripped Lilith's hand. 'We will be all right. The water will only come up so far.'

But I knew the tightness of her grip wasn't caused by worry about us, but for Amis, Rodden and the king. What if they'd been struggling with the king when the wave came in? Would they have known how fast it was advancing? It was too fast to outrun. Too powerful not to be inundated by.

The ashen sky grew even darker. A shrill, high scream pierced the air. I groaned, knowing my worst fear had been realised. Out of the gloom came the shapes of beating wings, and they were upon us before the soldiers could even draw their weapons.

The crowded battlements were at once in mayhem. A dozen brants swooped over our heads, harming riders with swords in their hands swinging at anything that moved. The courtiers, unarmed and unarmoured as they were, were easy targets. Blood spattered on the stones and people screamed and fell. Blood was trampled back and forth by panicked feet.

I grabbed Lilith around the waist and pulled her down. We huddled together, heads pressed against our knees, arms interlaced over each other's heads. If we stood we'd be cut down like the others, so could do nothing but cower and listen to the screaming. Soldiers bellowed orders but could barely be heard above the confusion.

I should get a weapon somehow and fight. But Lilith couldn't defend herself. 'We're going to wait for the right moment,' I said into Lilith's hair, close to her ear, 'and then we're going to run along the battlements and down the stairs.'

'We'll be drowned,' she wailed, not looking up.

'Don't be silly,' I replied. 'The cellars might be flooded, but not the whole palace.' I spoke with conviction but I couldn't know for sure. All I knew was that waves that came in had to go out again, and that staying huddled on the battlements was going to be far worse for our prospects than a few flooded rooms.

'All right,' she agreed. 'Tell me when.'

A hundred feet along the battlements I could see courtiers disappearing back down the stairs. Between us and that escape a battle was raging. More brants had appeared out of the falling ash and dropped harmings atop the walls. Having taken us by surprise the fighting was in their favour. Looking the other way there weren't any better prospects for Lilith and I. The parapet was crowded with harmings and soldiers and screaming courtiers.

It wasn't a good time, and it wasn't a bad time. There was too much confusion to time it well. I just knew I wanted to get Lilith off the battlements. 'Along to our left,' I said, getting into a crouch. 'Now. Go.' We stood, and we ran.

In the same moment a screaming brant descended towards us, talons first. Lilith half-turned at the scream, looked like she was going to scream herself, and then we grasped each other around the waist and flung ourselves down on our bellies. The talons snapped over our heads. There was a thud of feet as the brant's rider landed on the battlements.

'Go, run,' I urged Lilith, pulling her up and shoving her towards the stairway down into the palace. I

looked for a weapon. There were several dead courtiers around us, but none of them had been armed.
The nearest soldier was yards away.

The harming was stocky and armed with a sword,
and looked very mean. He surveyed the fighting with
pleasure, taking his time deciding where to launch
himself into the thick of it. Then he saw me, and his
smile caught. 'Don't I know you?' he asked, turning
to face me. I prayed Lilith had run like I'd told her
and was now descending the stairs with the others.

'I don't think so,' I replied. If he'd ever set eyes
on me it was probably to witness me doing something
not very nice to his friends.

'No, I do know you,' he insisted, but he was still
puzzled, as if he couldn't place my face.

'Ah, that's probably because I'm a harming,
too. Lost my weapon fighting all these Pergamians,'
I bluffed. I did look like a harming after all. I was
a harming. Just not a very good one by their standards. 'You don't have a spare sword about you, do
you? Then I could get back to the killing. And the
maiming.'

'Sorry, I …' His face changed. I saw the recognition bloom in his eyes.

Drat.

'I do know you. You're our ruddy queen.' He spat
the last word.

Was that any way to greet his ruler? I supposed
that since Garrick had died the loyalty to me had
died with him.

'You did this to us. You destroyed Lharmell. Oh, I'm going to enjoy killing you.' He raised his sword to strike.

I darted back as the sword swung in a wide arc, narrowly missing slicing open my belly from one side to the other. 'I'm still your queen, you know,' I protested.

'By whose laws? By whose orders?' he said.

'By – by the inheritance laws of Brivora. I am Garrick's heir.' I wasn't the slightest bit interested in becoming his queen, but if it meant he would put down his sword he could crown me this moment. The harming said something very rude about where I could stuff my Brivoran inheritance laws, and slashed again. The tip of the sword tore through fabric and bit into my left shoulder. I cried out, stumbled back and tripped over my own feet. An alarming quantity of blood seeped between my fingers where I held the wound. I had seen blood many times before, and always with equanimity. But there was, I thought, nothing quite so very red and very frightening as one's own blood in large amounts. The harming lifted his sword to stab me where I lay and I had a feeling I was about to see a great deal more of my own blood.

The seconds stretched and the harming didn't move. His nasty grin became strained, and then a cloudy tint glazed his eyes. A moment later, he keeled over.

I sat up in surprise, wondering what could possibly have come over him. It was then that I saw two arrows sprouting from his breastbone. They had come from behind me, and I turned. Lilith, her nightclothes stirring in the breeze and ash caught like cherry blossoms in her golden hair, was lowering a bow. Beyond her lay a dead archer, relieved of his weapon.

'I didn't know you could shoot,' I said, struggling to my feet.

'Amis thought it might be wise that I learn, considering where we live. All the ladies shoot for sport.' Her eyes avoided the dead harming and her face was very white.

With some effort, as every movement caused the wound in my shoulder to burn with pain, I hefted the harming's sword in my right hand and brandished it. It was for show more than anything. I didn't know how to fight with a sword. Sometime in the last few minutes the bells had begun to ring again. Soldiers were now pouring onto the battlements. Lilith and I made it back down into the palace without having to use our weapons again.

We made it to Lilith's bedchamber without seeing any signs of flooding. She sat me on the bed and tore my ripped shirt open to expose the wound in my shoulder.

'How do you feel?' she asked, examining the cut.

'All right. How do you feel?' Even though I was the wounded one I was more concerned about her. She'd never been in the midst of a battle before.

'Fine,' was the reply. Her voice was clipped and her face was still pale, and I thought that if

I made her talk anymore she might throw up or cry. She washed the cut, which turned out not to be very deep after all, and had only torn my skin and not cut into muscle. She bandaged it with a petticoat, one ear on the passageway behind her. At the sound of every pair of running feet outside the door her ears would prick up. I knew she was worried about Amis. I was worried too, about him and about Rodden.

'Not too tight,' I told Lilith. 'I need to be able to move my arm to shoot.'

'You can't shoot, you're wounded.'

'I'll be all right.'

Lilith flung the ripped petticoat onto the bed. 'And what about me?'

'The cellars might be flooded, but there'll be a safe place for you to –'

'So I'm supposed to cower inside, alone?' Her voice shook and I saw she was dangerously close to bursting into tears.

'Would you rather fight?' I asked, preferring challenge to sympathy. If I petted her with kind words she might succumb to her tears.

'Of course I wouldn't. I just want everything to be over and for Amis to be back.'

'I'm sure Renata wants that, too. Well, not Amis. But do you think she's weeping while she bandages her soldiers' wounds? She will be bandaging, you know. And losing sleep. And she hasn't got nearly as many people to help her.'

'Oh, shut-up, Fina,' Lilith said. But her eyes had cleared and she took a rallying breath. Her hands as she fastened my bandage were deft once more.

'Look, I won't go just yet,' I said, though all I wanted to do was head to the armoury and test out a bow with my wounded arm. Sitting idle meant there was too much time to think about Rodden and Amis and that awful wall of water. 'Shall we find the queen? She might have news of King Askar.' I didn't really believe that, but once we'd found the queen and seen that Lilith was more or less all right, I planned to leave her in the queen's motherly hands while I joined the soldiers on the battlements.

'All right,' Lilith said, and gave me a blouse to wear to replace the ruined one. As we were preparing to go, in swooped Griffin in a golden blur. She lighted on the bed and made urgent noises in the back of her throat. In her beak were several strands of black hair. She deposited them into my palm. They were three or four inches long, about the same length as Rodden's hair.

'Griffin, where did you get these?' I asked, clutching the strands.

There was the sound of tramping feet in the passage and two figures appeared at the door, out of breath. One had a hand to his head.

'I said I was coming, you dratted bird. We can't all fly,' Rodden grumbled.

Lilith cried out and ran to Amis, and they embraced. Rodden and I stayed where we were. I held up the hairs. 'I thought this was all that was left of you.'

'Griffin snatched you a memento before I drowned, you mean?' Rodden drawled, folding his arms. 'No, she doesn't have quite so romantic a nature. She did that just now in the hall because we weren't following along fast enough.'

'Ah. I did ask her to find you. Both of you.' Griffin was standing very erect on the bed, looking between us with her chest puffed with pride as if this was all her doing. Rodden followed my gaze and saw the basin of bloodied water. His eyes widened.

Before he could ask what was amiss, Lilith pulled out of her husband's embrace. 'Where is the king?' she asked.

Rodden looked at me. I looked at Amis. Lilith looked at all three of us in turn. 'We should find the queen,' Amis said, a little hoarsely, taking Lilith's hand and leading her out of the room.

When we were alone I said to Rodden, 'He's dead, isn't he?'

Rodden nodded his assent, and rubbed a hand across the back of his neck. 'We didn't get to him in time. We saw him on the beach from the top of the dunes, still in his nightclothes. He was very far out, further than the low tide mark. He had his palm up, as if ordering the water back. He still had it up as the wave crashed over him.'

For some reason Garrick's bloodied and dusty face, surrounded by fallen rocks, flashed through my mind. Two mad kings, dead of their own folly. 'Amis saw this too?' I asked.

'I'm afraid so. He looked so small. Wispy white hair blown about by the wind. But steady to the last. Then we had to turn back. We made it to the gatehouse before the wave crashed into the palace.' His eyes were drawn to the bloodied water again. 'What happened? Is one of you injured?' he asked. His eyes searched me.

I put a tentative hand to my shoulder. 'Just a nick. It happened on the battlements.'

'You were fighting? Why weren't you with your sister? Why didn't you have any armour on?'

I pursed my lips at his questions. 'I was with Lilith. After you and Amis left we were all told to get up to the battlements. Soldiers, courtiers, everyone.'

'Whose damn silly order was that?' Rodden nearly shouted.

'I don't know. One of the guards I think. The bells were ringing and everyone was so frightened. We could hear the wave coming. No one knew how high the water might break.'

'And nobody guessed that the harmings might choose that very moment to attack?'

'It's no good yelling at me,' I snapped.

He clenched his teeth. 'I'm sorry. But I saw the bodies laid out in the hall on my way to you, and it frightened me. I couldn't fathom how so many people had died in the short time Amis and I had been gone.'

'How many?'

'More than two dozen, most of them courtiers. There hasn't been time to put them in winding sheets and there is blood everywhere.'

'In the hall,' I echoed, thinking how not an hour hence they'd all been alive in that same place. Bodies had been put in the bailey the day before. It must be flooded.

'We must go to the battlements,' I said, heading for the door.

'But your arm –'

'Never mind my arm!'

CHAPTER EIGHTEEN

At the armoury we collected new weapons, having lost ours when Rodden's turret collapsed. I snuck a glance at his face, wondering whether he was thinking about everything he'd lost. But he only scowled at my look and handed me a crossbow. 'Here – can you load this with your injured arm?'

With my good arm I supported the heavy weapon and with the other I drew the string back as if I was notching a bolt. My shoulder came alive with pain and my arm shook. 'It's fine.'

'Liar. You're shaking.'

'It's winter. Now come on, or it will be winter here forever.'

Rodden chose us a spot on the south-western side of the battlements, saying it was dangerously unprotected.

'Dangerously dull, you mean. The fighting's on the northern side of the palace.'

'There's no side when the attack comes from the air.' And as if to prove his point two brants and riders suddenly rose up from behind the outer wall, and I was too busy shooting to complain about being away from the fighting.

We stayed atop the wall for several hours, firing at the brants as they banked past the wall, and the harmings that dropped onto the battlements to skirmish with the soldiers. Every attack was more or less a surprise due to the poor visibility. Between the fighting and the pain in my arm I had little time to look about me, but every now and then I cast a glance towards the city, still shrouded in fog and ash. I thought I saw flames in the gloom, and wondered what sort of devastation the wave had wreaked.

Two soldiers and a swordsman relieved us in the middle of the afternoon and, in nearly too much pain to carry my own crossbow, I limped after Rodden down from the battlements. He took me back to Lilith and Amis's rooms and piled our weapons on the table. 'I trust they'll forgive the liberty at a time like this,' he muttered. He helped me out of my armour, and then gave a little hiss when he saw the blood that had soaked the shirt beneath. 'You need a surgeon.'

'Lilith didn't say it needed stitches.' But I was too tired to argue any more and he marched me out of the room.

As we were in the midst of a battle there was, naturally, a queue for the surgeon. I had never had occasion to visit him before but knew him to be a shortish middle-aged man in a leather cap who kept a suite of rooms just above in the north-eastern cellars. Two young women with hair swathed in blood-spattered linen aprons were moving among the soldiers, assessing their need for attention.

Rodden looked around first with annoyance at the crowd, and then pity as the groans of the mortally wounded met his ears. We waited about a quarter of an hour until it became clear that my cut wasn't going to warrant anyone's attention for a very long time. Rodden went to have a word with one of the young women. She nodded, then came back with a few things on a small wooden tray.

'Come on,' he said to me after thanking her. 'Let's go to the kitchens.'

I looked suspiciously at the tray, but was glad to leave all that suffering, far worse than mine, behind me.

In the kitchens I sat atop a stool by one of the smaller hearths that was still lit while Rodden busied himself around me. Across the cavernous grey room, the main hearth was being repaired from the damage by the morning's quake. Too tired to do anything else, I watched the men re-bricking the chimney.

'Drink this.' Rodden handed me a steaming mug. 'Willow bark tea, for the pain.' He ripped open the sleeve of my shirt and took the bloodied bandage off. The tea was very bitter, but I drank it down. The pain ebbed after a few minutes, and I turned my attention to what Rodden was doing. He had a basin of hot water, a small bottle of something, and a curved needle. He was rolling his sleeves up.

'What do you think you're going to do with that?'

'You do need stitches.'

'How would you know?'

'I just do.'

'Rot. Have you ever given anyone stitches?'

He began washing his hands in the basin. 'I've read about it.'

I gave a barking laugh. 'You've read about it. I suppose you read how to make this terrible tea.'

'It's not supposed to taste good. It's medicine.'

With a clean piece of linen he sponged down my shoulder, dabbing on the contents of the little bottle.

'Ow. What's that?'

'St John's wort, to prevent infection.'

'Well, that's plenty of surgeoning from you. I feel better already.' I made to get up.

He put a restraining hand on my arm. 'It won't heal unless I stitch it up. Two knots, maybe three, that's all.'

I looked at him angrily. 'Have you every stabbed yourself in the finger with a needle? Do you remember how much that hurts?'

He had the decency to at least wince. 'I know. It will hurt. But you will heal quickly this way, and who know what might happen in the coming ... Who knows what might happen,' he finished.

'What do you think might happen?' I asked, watching him thread the needle with silk and use tongs to dip it into the water boiling on the hearth.

Rodden didn't answer for a moment. He waited for the needle to cool, and then got to work. I couldn't say what he did because I looked firmly the other way and tried not to writhe about too much. In not very long at all I was sweating and cursing and had tears coursing down my cheeks, but from pain rather than from weeping.

'We might have to flee,' he said quietly when he'd finished, and handed me a clean piece of linen to wipe my face.

'What, all of us? Abandon the palace?'

'Yes.'

The harmings and Lharmellins would take it. Things would start all over again. 'But we're holding them off,' I protested. Across the wound in my shoulder were three neat knots, and the top of my arm felt very tight and immovable.

Instead of answering Rodden began bandaging my arm. Finally, he said quietly, 'It will be up to the king if that happens. But I'm sure he's thinking about it.'

'The king?' For a moment I thought he was referring to King Askar. 'Oh, Amis. Of course. What unhappy circumstances for him.'

'I think he must have prepared all his life for the circumstances to be unhappy ones. Becoming king always meant his father's death.' He helped me up. 'Come on, let's find you somewhere to rest.'

CHAPTER NINETEEN

'Very neat work,' Lilith said to Rodden, bandaging my shoulder again and doing up my shirt. I would have done it myself but as I'd slept the afternoon away my left arm had stiffened and it hurt to move it even the tiniest bit. 'My own stitchery was never so neat.'

Rodden had installed me in an empty room with a bed, a fireplace and a table and chairs. I'd fallen asleep while Rodden had sat by the narrow window, one foot braced on a wooden chest, sharpening yelbar points. I found the rasp of metal on whetstone soothing though it hadn't always been that way. Before I'd fallen asleep I'd listened and thought fiercely, *Rodden's back. He's really back.*

Sometime in the afternoon he'd gone to the battlements again and fought alongside Amis. He'd brought the new king and Lilith to me as the sun had set and the fighting ended. Strange red light had glowed in the west, the ash in the air making the sunset blaze. Now it was evening and the four of us occupied the small space; Rodden standing with his back to the fire, Amis slumped on the wooden chest, me sitting on a chair and Lilith hovering over me. Only Lilith had the energy to do much talking. She'd been ensconced in a room somewhere with the queen all day with nothing but fretting to pass the hours. Rodden gave her a weak smile.

'How goes the fighting?' I asked Amis.

He was still in his armour with his hand resting on his sword hilt, as if he expected to draw it at any moment. Exhausted, he went to pass a hand over his face but saw that it was still gauntleted. Lilith went to him and began undoing buckles.

His face was grim. 'It is how I always thought it would be. Except that I am giving the orders, not receiving them.'

'Amis, I am sorry. I mean, your majesty,' I said.

Amis winced. 'Don't call me that. Not in here. I am still not used to it from the men.'

'They kept coming all day, without a break,' Rodden said, meaning the harmings.

I didn't like the bleakness in his eyes. It was only the second day and it seemed like he was giving up already. I wanted to tell him to buck himself up – at least he had the use of all his arms and legs. I'd probably be cooped up with all the ladies on the morrow, oblivious to everything that was happening. Frustrated, I kicked at the table leg. 'Ow,' I muttered.

'Fina, what's the matter?' Lilith asked, sitting down beside me.

'Only that I can't fight tomorrow. My arm's too stiff to load my crossbow.'

'We are well protected,' Amis said. 'There were few casualties this afternoon, and many men to fight tomorrow.'

'That's not the point,' I said. 'I feel completely useless.'

For a moment we were all silent. Then Lilith said, 'Could you fight if you had someone to load your crossbow?'

I thought about this. I could brace and fire the contraption with my right hand. As long as I didn't move my left I would be perfectly capable. 'Yes, I think I could. But it's a waste of a soldier to do nothing but notch bolts for me.'

'I'll do it,' she offered.

We all stared at her.

'What? Don't you think I could?' she said angrily.

Amis grinned. 'You sounded just like your sister when you said that.'

'I don't doubt that you could, Lilith. Only that you would want to.' I tried not to sound too eager. Between the two of us we could make up one decent fighter. But Lilith didn't like dangerous undertakings. She liked calm and for everything to be in its place.

'It wasn't so bad on the battlements this morning when I shot that –' She broke off, looking pale.

Amis and Rodden stared at her. It seemed they hadn't heard that Lilith had saved my life.

'All right, it was quite dreadful,' she conceded. 'But what's worse is sitting and hoping and worrying. I want to do it,' she finished, glaring at all of us in turn.

Amis looked at me. 'What do you think, Zeraphina?'

'We would be very vulnerable to attack. Neither of us can wield a sword or a staff.'

'Do you have an axe in the armoury?' Rodden asked Amis.

Amis widened his eyes. 'Yes, why? Can you fight with an axe?'

I shuddered, remembering how 'Raufo' had decapitated a harming in front of me. 'Yes, he can. We'd be well protected if Rodden had a two-headed axe.'

'We have such a weapon,' Amis replied. He looked at his wife. 'It is up to you then.'

'I have already said I would, haven't I?' she replied a little peevishly, to hide her nervousness, I suspected.

Amis stood. 'Shall we go and look for that axe?' he asked Rodden.

The pair of them quit the room. Lilith was very quiet and round-eyed, staring at the fire but not seeing the flames, I was sure. A short while later a kitchen girl knocked at the door with a tray and I took the food from her gratefully, guessing that Amis or Rodden had sent it to us.

We ate bread and cold mutton and pieces of orange. There was a mug of willow bark tea as well, and I drank it down as soon as it had cooled a little.

'Would you like to lie down?' I asked Lilith when we were done, as she was still pensive, but fading fast.

'I shan't sleep,' she told me as I led her to the bed, but she fell asleep in the time it took me to snuff all but one of the candles. I watched her for a little while, not sleepy, wondering where she found her courage. It wasn't easy fighting on the battlements, as she'd seen. If she hadn't shot that harming earlier in the morning I would have doubted, if not her courage, then the sense of her offer. But she knew what it would be like, and still she wanted to help.

A few hours later the door opened quietly and Rodden stood in the doorway. He smiled when he saw Lilith asleep on the bed. I was sitting at the little table again, just thinking, feeling the sleepiness creep back slowly and knowing I should return to bed myself soon.

'Have you got everything you need for tomorrow?' I asked quietly.

He nodded. 'Would you like me to carry her to her own bed?'

'No, there's room for both of us here. She needs to sleep.' I looked at her, golden hair wreathing her head. 'She saved my life today.'

'What happened?'

I shrugged with my good shoulder. 'A harming got me, and she yanked a bow off a dead archer and shot it.'

'She's very different, isn't she?'

I considered this. 'The last time we were in Pergamia she was very haughty and self-conscious. I think she felt everyone was measuring her up as future queen. This morning I think she realised how quickly everything can be taken away from her. So she's just getting on with things.' I smiled. 'Amis said she sounded just like me, earlier. Actually, she sounded just like she did when she was little.'

'You are your mother's daughters,' he replied wryly. He looked like he wanted to come into the room, and I waited, seeing what he would so. But he only bid me goodnight, saying he would bunk down on the floor in Amis's chambers, and closed the door gently behind him.

The room was illuminated by candlelight when I was shaken awake. Lilith was standing over me and pressed something soft into my hands. 'I got us some fresh clothes. There's a basin of hot water on the table.' She was already dressed and had placed a mug of willow bark tea on the table.

I got up. 'What time is it?' I asked, sipping on my tea. My wounded arm was still stiff and sore. I wasn't going to be able to fight without Lilith's help.

'About half an hour till dawn.'

I washed and dressed while she cut up bread and fruit. Like mine, Lilith's shirt and trousers were a dull brown and she was shod in riding boots. Her long hair was bound up and wrapped in more rough cloth. 'Rodden and Amis just went up to the battlements,' she said around a mouthful of bread, and then chewed hard. 'Stale,' she muttered. 'The ovens still aren't working properly. Rodden has your crossbow.'

I shoved some bread and an apple into my pocket. 'We should go.'

In the pre-dawn light, Rodden was limbering up. He wore full armour, like Amis, and the great two-headed axe was resting against the crennelations. It looked very sharp, and very heavy. Amis was a little distance away talking to the archers and soldiers.

Lilith knelt on the stones and began sorting through bolts and points. She had a bow to hand in case she needed to defend herself. We decided that the best thing for her to do was crouch low by the wall beside me, doing her best to keep out of sight. But the passing archers noted the small form and slim hands sorting through the arrows, and it amused me to watch their eyes widen and their hasty bows as they recognised their new queen.

Rodden strapped the axe to his back in easy reach and took up his bow. His eyes looked north. I stood by him, seeing patches of palest yellow break through the thick cloud cover. Dawn was upon us.

'Are you going to be all right?' he asked me in a low voice, passing me the loaded crossbow.

It was just light enough to be held in one arm. 'This is where I need to be,' I replied. He nodded, his eyes searching the heavens.

The battlements became very still and silent. All eyes were on the drifting ash and smoke in the sky and it was as if everyone held their breath. I looked down to where Lilith was crouched and caught her eye. She looked tense, but resolute.

The minutes stretched on and the sky lightened. I began to think there would be no fighting that day after all, when a thin, high scream pierced the air. Instantly, several more cries sounded in answer, and wings thundered on the air.

Amis had disappeared along the wall into the gloom, but I heard his bellow. 'Draw.'

The birds were still invisible, but we could hear them. The air was filled with the sound of beating wings.

'How many are there?' asked Rodden, bow drawn and aimed at a steep angle. The point wavered left and right as he tried to pinpoint a single one.

'I can't tell. They seem to be flying … *around* us.' Every time I thought a bird was going to burst through the ashy air and attack it whirred past, going sunwise. Seconds stretched into minutes. The brants were close enough to attack, but still they didn't. And as we waited it seemed like their numbers grew. They were circling us, waiting.

'*Fire*,' came the order. The sound of loosed bow-strings filled the air. There was a pause as the archers notched. I handed my fired crossbow to Lilith. With deft fingers she fitted a bolt.

There must have been a signal, but we neither heard it nor saw it. The brants plunged out of the fog, talons-first, and screaming.

Rodden swore, threw his bow aside and drew his axe, swinging it in a deadly arc. The brant that had been reaching to tear him apart with its talons was manoeuvred out of harm's way. Lilith made a sound like she wanted to scream, and then remembered that she wasn't meant to draw attention to herself. She still held the crossbow, and with her other hand she grabbed me by the hand and pulled me down.

It was as if night had fallen once more. The air was thick with the giant birds, all screaming and diving as they flocked over our heads. Upon their backs were Lharmellins, not harmings. Their black robes were streaming behind them, hoods thrown back to reveal ghoulish faces, pitted eyes glowing pale blue in the gloom. Each wielded a wickedly long sword. It was a fearsome sight to one who was accustomed to their appearance. I could only guess how the soldiers and archers felt, face to face with this inhuman army for the first time.

Lilith elbowed me, terror in her eyes but with sense enough in their depths. She gripped three crossbow bolts in her hands, each tipped with yel-bar. '*Fire*, would you?' She had to yell in my ear to be heard over the sound of clashing weapons and the screams of the dying.

I realised that she'd handed me the crossbow but I'd been too frozen by the sounds and sights of the battle to notice. Still crouched beside her I took aim at a Lharmellin as it wheeled by, and loosed. My aim was poor and the bolt arced harmlessly into the fog.

While Lilith reloaded I took a deep breath and took stock of my surroundings, taking in the chaos as dispassionately as I could. My shoulder hurt and restricted my activities, but that was why Lilith was at my side. The two of us couldn't defend ourselves in hand to hand combat, but that was why Rodden was by our side, and many other soldiers beside. The air might be in turmoil, but the battlements were ours. I realised I was frightened by the Lharmellins, more than I had been by the harmings. Their faces were inscrutable. It was impossible to tell what they were going to do or what they wanted, except that they were hungry. Garrick had lived in closed quarters with these creatures for many years. It was little wonder he'd lost his compassion.

As Lilith handed me the loaded crossbow a Lharmellin slid from brant-back and landed twenty feet from where we huddled. Very thin and standing a head taller than Rodden, it looked about it for a moment. Then it grasped a felled solider at its feet by the lapels, hauled it up and began to drink. The soldier wasn't quite dead, and I saw his eyes roll. With a horrified cry, I loosed the yelbar-tipped bolt. The missile buried itself in the creature's shoulder. A high-pitched noise somewhere between a scream and a gurgle rent the air, followed by the sound of something flammable igniting, and then the thing crumpled up in a heap on the stones.

Lilith was breathing hard but her hands were steady as she reloaded for me. Where we sat, below head height, I was best suited to aiming at the Lharmellins who landed on the battlements. It was a difficult undertaking as we were surrounded by friends as well as foes, and I was terrified of shooting one of our own soldiers. I didn't hurry, though, and without a weapon of her own to see to, Lilith had time to look about us.

'There, to the right. I saw a black cloak between those archers.'

I saw where she pointed, but was loathe to fire into the midst of fighting men. Seconds passed as I waited for my shot. The swoop of a brant gave me my chance – the archers dove for cover and the Lharmellin stood out in stark relief against the grey stone. I fired, and that same screaming gurgle filled the air.

Beside us Rodden had given up on his bow and relied exclusively on his axe to keep the airborne brants and riders at bay. One bird dogged him continually, and I had an idea to do something about either the brant or rider when the opportunity arose.

'Do you see any Lharmellins on the battlements?' I asked Lilith.

She craned her neck. 'Not now.'

'Tell me the second you do.' I angled my eyes and my weapon skywards, keeping Rodden in my peripheral vision lest I got carried away and shot him. The Lharmellin played the brant over Rodden's head like a cat baiting a mouse, attempting to wear him out. The bird was fast for such a mighty animal and trained to respond in an instant.

'Fina, there is a Lharmellin on the battlements.'

'How far?' I asked, not looking away from my quarry.

'Forty feet.'

The brant swept over our heads in a figure eight. The Lharmellin rider swung its sword at Rodden and grinned, as if play fighting.

Lilith's voice rose a little. 'Oh, stars, it's spotted us. It's coming toward us. Thirty feet.'

Still I kept my crossbow trained upward.

'Fina, it is *coming for us.*' Lilith's voice rose in a shriek and she shrunk against the wall. I could see the Lharmellin now out of the corner of my eye, a dark figure fast approaching, sword in hand. It would cut through both of us in one stroke while Rodden was occupied with the brant overhead.

But Rodden had heard this exchange. We kept our eyes on the wheeling brant overhead, but I knew what was in his mind as surely as if he'd spoken it aloud.

The Lharmellin was three long strides away and raised his sword to strike. In an instant Rodden whirled, as I knew he would. He crossed in front of us as he spun, both hands gripping the axe. The Lharmellin on the battlements faltered, but it was too late. Overhead the rider took the bait. He wheeled the bird directly over my head, urging his bird to dive at Rodden while his attention was elsewhere, giving me just enough time to take aim at the bird's heart. I loosed my bolt as Rodden's blade cut through our attacker.

The bird crashed onto the battlements at our feet. Lilith covered her face and peeked between her fingers, too startled to take the crossbow from me. Rodden dispatched the rider where it struggled beneath the felled bird, and flashed me a grim smile.

Lilith, aghast, looked between us. 'You both knew what was going to happen, but I thought we were going to die.'

'Yes, but only for a moment,' I consoled her. She finally took the crossbow from me, yanking it out of my hands.

Rodden looked at the dead brant. 'This isn't a good place for us. I can't get to you if you're attacked.'

Lilith scrambled into a crouch in a second, anxious to get away from the dead bird. 'We'll move.'

More hesitant about the idea of running into a battle I could barely see, I looked up and down the ramparts. 'Are you sure you're not tiring?' I asked Lilith. She shook her head, gathering up the bolts at her feet.

Rodden was pointing to the left. 'Just up a little further –' He broke off as a brant dived out of the sky and swooped at him. He ducked just in time but I saw how close the talons had come to slicing into his neck. The bird wheeled and came back for another pass. Rodden hefted his axe.

'We'll stay here for a moment,' I said to Lilith.

The rider of this brant wasn't a Lharmellin. He was the first harming rider I'd seen all morning. Rodden was careful to avoid the diving bird and the out-thrust talons, but he wasn't trying to attack it, either. He was staring at the rider as if too stunned to act. The bird lit upon the battlements, the rider unconcerned about the battle raging around him. He was a large man, and there was something familiar about his broad face and deep set eyes.

'Fina –' Lilith started.

'Hush,' I muttered, seeing Rodden lower his axe to gaze at the figure. I recognised him now. Servilock. He turned to cast a look of greeting in my direction, one that burned with hate. When I'd last seen him he'd been delivering me to Garrick. I wondered if he was regretting not killing me then.

But it was clear I wasn't his first objective in coming to the palace this morning. He turned to Rodden and opened his mouth to speak. There was a loud twang and then a whistle, and he froze in place. Slowly he pitched forward and toppled from the saddle. Alarmed, the brant flapped its wings and danced this way and that on the stones. Finally, realising it was free, it launched itself into the air and flew from the battlements, leaving its crumpled master behind.

Rodden turned to stare at Lilith. I stared at Lilith. She was holding the crossbow aloft, looking between us with a guilty expression. 'Did I do something wrong?' she asked. We were too shocked to speak, and Lilith covered her mouth. 'Did I just kill one of your friends?'

Rodden recovered first. 'No, no, don't think that. We just – it's just –' The blank shock on his face turned to relief.

'It just shouldn't have been that easy,' I finished. 'Or rather, he shouldn't have been so stupid as to land on the battlements among his enemies. Foolish, and very conceited.'

Rodden knelt over the body of his old master. 'He's not dead.' With a sharp tug he pulled the bolt from the harming's side and examined it. 'It's a plain bolt.' He threw the point to the ground.

'Oh, I am sorry.' Lilith looked so confused by all this that I sensed she was about to cry. I wasn't sure whether Rodden was happy that Servilock was still alive either. We watched as he hailed two soldiers.

'Take this harming to the surgeon, and keep him under guard at all times. He's extremely dangerous, and he's my prisoner.'

We watched the soldier's take Servilock underneath the arms and drag him away.

'I must have picked up a plain bolt by mistake,' Lilith said, still not knowing whether she'd done right or not.

Rodden came and knelt down next to her, taking her hands in his. 'Thank you, Lilith. I didn't know what I was going to do when I saw who that harming was. We have a great deal of history between us. I suppose he thought I would want to listen to what he had to say and that would be enough to protect him. He was always a very arrogant man.'

'Maybe he wanted to ...' she half-shrugged, 'apologise?'

Rodden's mouth quirked in a smile. 'I doubt it. And I don't think I wanted to hear anything that man had to say anyway. Now, do you want to go inside?'

Lilith looked around her at the fighting soldiers, the wheeling shapes in the sky, the blood-spattered stones. 'No. I want to help.'

Rodden looked a question at me.

The ache in my arm was a dull throb and I would have liked some willow bark tea, but distraction would do. 'I'm fine, too. We need to find a better position though.'

The three of us took up our weapons and crept low along the battlements. The captain of the guard, Hoggit, was standing at the end of a row of archers, and he paused in his bellowing of *draw, aim, fire!* to direct us thirty feet further along, saying, 'There's an unprotected spot that could use some fillin'.'

Lilith and I crouched down again, my sister muttering, 'Yelbar, plain,' to herself as she sorted through the bolts, seemingly determined not to get them muddled again.

I watched Rodden as he scanned the skies, face unreadable. I couldn't guess at what he might do with Servilock now that he had him prisoner. He might be secretly wishing that Lilith had fired a yelbar point after all if he truly didn't want to speak with him. What I did know was that I was grateful that he'd seen my sister's distress and took pains to reassure her that she'd done the right thing after all.

I took the loaded crossbow that she offered me and looked at the sky. After a while I said to Rodden, 'You know, I wouldn't mind taking a brant or two away from the Lharmellins.'

He glanced at me a moment. 'You're thinking of your mother,' he guessed.

I nodded. I was thinking of Renata. Anything might be happening in Amentia and I had no way of aiding her. But if we survived this siege and had brants, we could reach her quickly.

Rodden laid his axe aside and crouched next to me. 'All right, then,' he murmured.

The next time a brant and rider flew overhead we reached out to it with our minds, calling it down to the battlements. It wasn't easy. Brants stubbornly obeyed their riders. But part a brant from a harming or Lharmellin and it would be happy to obey the next one. The Lharmellin who rode this brant seem annoyed that its mount was becoming confused. It hadn't noticed Rodden and me below, and when the brant dipped low enough Rodden darted out and took hold of the bridle. Ready with my crossbow I shot the baffled Lharmellin.

Rodden shouted for a pair of soldiers with swords to flank Lilith and me, then mounted the brant and flew it down to the bailey. Five minutes later he was back, jogging along the battlements, slightly out of breath but pleased with the result. 'Another?' he asked me, and I nodded.

We continued on in this vein into the afternoon, and soon I could hear the dozen brants we'd captured squawking in the bailey below. Not only did I preferring capturing the magnificent birds to killing them, but I was thinking of every additional soldier I could take to Renata's aid.

Eventually Hoggit marched a half-dozen archers to the place on the battlements we occupied and snapped at the three of us, 'You are relieved. Go and take some refreshment.'

'What is it?'

Lilith was staring at me, her eyes tired and jaw working methodically on the piece of bread she chewed. We sat at a trestle in the great hall, the low murmurs of exhausted soldiers around us. My shoulder was aching and I couldn't yet face the parsnip soup in front of me.

'Was it always like this?' she asked.

'What do you mean?'

Her eyes slid from mine and looked around the hall. 'When you and Rodden went into Lharmell. Those creatures are …' She shook slightly, rubbing her arms. 'I still feel so cold. When they looked at me I felt like there were ice crystals forming in my blood.'

I knew exactly what she meant. 'I have never got used to seeing Lharmellins,' I said, and wrapped my hands around the earthenware bowl in front of me, absorbing its warmth even if I wasn't ready to eat. 'But I only saw them half a dozen times. And only ever in Lharmell.'

'What does it mean that they have come here?'

I shook my head. 'I don't know.'

Rodden appeared and placed a steaming mug before me.

'Willow bark?' I asked hopefully.

He nodded and sat down. I pushed my bowl toward him. 'Here, I can't eat yet.' While I drank I saw Lilith sneaking looks at Rodden.

Guessing the direction of her thoughts, I asked him, 'What will you do about Servilock?'

Rodden looked up. There were dark shadows beneath his eyes, but they'd lost that hopeless expression I'd seen the previous day. 'I hadn't really thought about it.' He was silent a long moment. Then he asked us, 'Was it just me, or did it seem like there were fewer attacks as the afternoon wore on?'

'Yes, I think so. Don't you, Fina?'

I thought carefully, but I'd been so distracted by pain and trying to control brants that I hadn't thought about whether their numbers were slowing. I was burning to ask Rodden what he thought the next day would bring, but he couldn't know any more than I could.

CHAPTER TWENTY

The torchlight flickered in Lilith's eyes. It was predawn and the three of us had taken up our position on the battlements once more. This time Amis had joined us, and we stood silently, straining to hear beyond the cloud and ash that shrouded the castle.

Below came the gentle scuffing and hisses of a flock of brants waking from a night in the bailey. Along the battlements were soft metallic sounds of the soldier's armour and weapons as they shifted their feet. Everyone was keyed up, straining for the sounds of the approaching enemy, and dreading it at the same time.

The sky lightened. Everyone seemed to hold their breath. This was the time the previous day when the Lharmellins had attacked. The minutes crawled by.

There was a sharp, loud clang, and I started, but it was only Rodden slamming the butt of his axe against the stones in frustration. 'Where are they?' he muttered.

Amis put a hand on his friend's shoulder. 'When you three left the battlements yesterday there were still several hours of sunlight. But the attacks dwindled and stopped before sunset.'

Rodden didn't respond to this, still looking grave. Amis nodded to us and resumed his patrol of the battlements.

I sat with my legs straight out in front of me, back resting against the wall, but kept my crossbow aloft. The stones were very cold beneath me. Rodden, irritated and fidgety, paced back and forth and stared into the fog as if he could pierce it with the will of his gaze.

Several hours passed in uneasy silence. Uneasy for most – Lilith fell asleep against my shoulder, huddled into me for warmth. To keep myself amused, and to prevent myself from snapping at Rodden to keep *still*, for goodness' sake, I watched the swirling patterns that the fog and ash made over my head. Unseen and unfelt, there were currents in the air that blew it in swirling eddies, creating pleasing shapes and ripples.

Even though I had been staring for many hours, it was a shock to me when the sun came out. Rodden stopped his pacing and stared at the sky. I jerked upright with such haste that I woke Lilith.

'What is it? Are we under attack?' She half reached for the crossbow, but stopped when she saw that it was still loaded and lay forgotten in my lap.

The sunshine grew stronger, warming my upturned face. As we watched, blue patches appeared in the sky. The colour was a shock after so many grey days. Rodden turned to me, and he must have been thinking the same thing as he said, 'When was the last time,' he said slowly, 'that you saw the sun in a blue sky?'

Lilith helped me to stand, and bit by bit beneath the clearing sky, the cold ebbed from my body. It felt like it had been forever, though I knew it hadn't been so very long, really. But there was something significant about the sunshine that morning. It cast its spell on everyone on the battlements. Weapons were laid down. Hunched shoulders were thrown back as if great weights had been relieved.

I looked at Rodden and saw there was something glimmering in his pale blue eyes. Something hopeful. 'Too long,' I said. 'Far too long.'

'Stop doing that. You'll break your stitches,' Rodden said.

I paused, left arm held aloft mid-rotation. The bandage was off and I was testing how the wound felt. It was the following morning and we sat in the great hall over a late breakfast, sunlight streaming through the high windows. Grinning at Rodden, I said, 'How would you know? Did you read it in a book?'

He cast his eyes to the rafters but I could see a smile glimmering around his mouth. He wore no armour now, though he had donned it over his clean white shirt at dawn, just in case. The morning had begun bright and clear and had grown very warm very quickly. A brisk breeze had blown the last of the ash haze out to sea and from atop the battlements we had seen the city once more. Word had come that the city had survived the worst of the wave, the high walls holding up against the torrent.

To the north the horizon was still hazy. We couldn't know what was happening in that direction, but we could hope.

'My arm feels much better this morning,' I ventured. 'I think I could ride.'

He gave me a sharp look. 'Really? A horse you mean?' But he knew I didn't mean a horse.

'I have to know what's happening in Amentia,' I replied.

His face became serious. 'I know. So do I.'

'But?' I asked. A sudden fear gripped me. Perhaps Rodden didn't want to go anywhere with me anymore. Our friendship seemed to have taken some steps towards a reconciliation, but there was still so much between us.

'Servilock,' he said. 'He's a prisoner here. Hoggit tells me he's been asking to see me.'

I felt a rush of relief. Of course. 'Do you want to see him?'

He sighed. 'I don't know. Perhaps Lilith should have been minding her bolts a little more closely after all.'

'He's Amis's prisoner, really. What does Amis want you to do? What would King Aksar have done?'

'Askar would have had him executed. He's an enemy of Brivora. But Amis has said he will leave the decision up to me.'

I remembered something that Rodden had told me once. It felt like a lifetime away now, but I heard the words as clearly in my head as I did then. *It is not the same, killing in cold blood.* But Servilock had caused Rodden unspeakable pain, so perhaps it wasn't so cold after all.

'Do you want revenge?' I asked.

'I don't know what I want. But I should see him.' He paused, and then looked like he wanted to say something more.

'What is it?'

Reaching out, he took my hand in both of his. His grasp was warm and comforting. 'I know I don't have the right to ask this. But will you come with me?'

I thought for a moment. 'I don't know ...' I began, not knowing how to say what I wanted to say.

Rodden looked away, trying to hide his disappointment.

'I don't know,' I continued, 'if I can go on not forgiving you.'

He looked up, studying my face. His hands tightened on mine. Then a small smiled formed. 'Are you saying, Zeraphina, in your indirect and stubborn way, that you forgive me?'

I sniffed. 'Perhaps.'

'What has brought me back into your good graces?'

I was tempted to shrug and simply hold onto his hand, letting all that had happened go unsaid. There were so many reasons to forgive him. But there had been one moment in particular that had changed everything for me, and he deserved to know. 'I saw what you saw.'

'What do you mean?'

'When you were Raufo. You didn't trust me to tell me who you were all those months, and when I found out I was so angry. There couldn't be one good reason you would lie to me for so long.' I took a deep breath. 'But when you took me with you to Amentia and we were so close we were like one person, I saw myself in your mind. It wasn't me you didn't trust. I was so far from being myself that I may as well have been a different person. And you hated that.'

'I didn't hate anything about you,' he said, voice hoarse. 'How could I?'

'You hated what had become of me.'

'If I hated anything, it was what I had done to you.'

I held even more tightly to his hand. 'I never told you how brave you were to go back down that tunnel. It's only because I want to be as brave as you that I can ask you this. Will you come with me to Amentia?'

'You have always been brave.'

'Is that a yes?'

A smile spread across his face. 'And impatient. And stubborn.'

I pulled my hand from his and punched him softly on the arm. 'Shut up and just tell me, would you?'

He stood, swept an elaborate bow before me, and said, 'Yes, your highness.'

Servilock was brought out into the bailey in chains. There was only Rodden and I and Amis present, and the soldiers that escorted him. And a flock of tethered brants. Servilock favoured one side as he walked, and I could see stiff white bandages beneath his torn clothes.

The brants stirred and squawked their recognition as he approached. The sun was lengthening the shadows in the bailey, the shapes of the crennelations atop the battlements stretched across the muddy ground. We stood half in shadow and half out of it.

'What was it you came to tell me?' Rodden asked as the harming was brought to a halt before us.

Servilock looked faintly amused. 'I didn't come to tell you anything. I only came to see.'

Rodden frowned. 'But you've been asking for me.'

'I wanted to be sure I had one last look at my fine young pupil before I died. My greatest creation.'

'What sort of creation turns against its master?' I asked.

Servilock gave me a frank look. 'One whose master has failed. I have been trying to work out just when that was. I think I erred over your family.'

Rodden shifted. 'Are you saying that you were wrong for what you made me do?'

'Oh, indeed. It was too much, too soon. I should have been more circumspect – perhaps one at a time rather than all at once. Alas, all becomes clear with hindsight.' There was no goading in his tone, only the vague regret of someone who has made a foolish but trivial mistake. He paused for a moment, perhaps replaying the most painful events in Rodden's life to see if he could have changed the outcome in any way. 'It matters not now. I have reconciled myself with my fate. But where is the yelbar dagger? Or will you behead me with that great axe of yours? Where is it?' He cast his eyes about the bailey, looking for the objects that would end his life.

The tension in Rodden's shoulders suddenly eased. 'You are reconciled,' he echoed faintly. 'King Amis has told me that I should serve justice as I see fit. You are an enemy of Pergamia and the law permits the severest of punishments.'

'Yes, yes,' Servilock said, as if impatient to be getting on with things. 'Execution, I know.'

'The law permits it, but I'm not bound to submit to it.'

'What?'

'Since I murdered my family at your behest, I have killed only to protect myself and my friends against my enemies. But you stand before me in chains. You are no longer my enemy.'

I don't know who was more startled, Servilock or myself. There was no one in the world who had caused Rodden more pain, and if he'd wished to see

Servilock die no one could have faulted his wishes. Servilock was a dangerous, hateful man.

'I will be executed,' Servilock ground out. 'It is my wish.'

'I relinquish you into the king's merciful hands.'

'Merciful?' Servilock said. 'It would be a mercy to die!'

'Yes, it would. But I am sick of death,' Rodden replied.

Across the bailey the brants stirred, straining at their tethers. I saw Servilock glance at them too, and the fury on his face slipped for a moment, becoming fierce concentration. A brant broke free. It spread its great sooty wings and opened its beak in a shrill, high scream.

Servilock smiled a victorious smile at Rodden. 'I will take my death,' the harming said.

There wasn't time enough to stop it. The bird launched itself across the bailey and Amis cried to his men holding Servilock to fall back. The brant grasped the harming in its talons and Servilock fell to the ground with a thud. There was the sound of bones breaking and a strangled, gurgling scream, and then the brant's wings drew around its prey to shield it from anything that might try to take it away.

Rodden turned to me, his face ashen. Even the battle-weary soldiers looked queasy.

It took me several minutes to persuade the brant to stop eating Rodden's former master. When it finally lifted its bloody head I caught it by the bridle and led it back to the other birds, trying not to look too closely at what remained of Servilock. There seemed to be several pieces.

When I came back Amis was looking at the brants, horrified. 'What made it do that?'

'He asked it to,' I replied. 'He knew it was all over for him and Lharmell, and he wanted to die.' I took Rodden's hand. 'I'm sorry,' I said, not sure what I was apologising for. Possibly for Servilock himself.

He gave a small shake of his head. 'Perhaps it is better this way. I just couldn't give the order myself. I've had enough. More than enough.'

I led him away, listening to the quiet that surrounded the palace once more. The bells had fallen silent. The battlements were empty. Sunlight fell through the unguarded arrow slits. There had been enough and perhaps it was over, for Pergamia, at least. But my thoughts were already retreating from this place and flying far over the continent, to Amentia.

CHAPTER TWENTY-ONE

It took three days to reach the castle at Amentia by brant. From the air the squat grey stone walls looked as much as they always had. I'd braced myself for billowing dark grey cloud and rivers of blood, but from as high as a crow – or in this case, brant – flies, there was nothing alarming about the vista below as we spiralled in to land. We were alone, Rodden and I, having decided it would be quicker to fly just the two of us and return for soldiers if we needed them rather than try and control a dozen brants with human riders.

It had been hard to leave Lilith in Pergamia, but I'd promised to send news by brant as soon as I reached the castle. 'You're needed here,' I'd said to her quietly when I'd seen her anguished face. 'Amis will be relying on you now he's king. He's lost his father and has had no time to come to terms with all the changes that are happening.'

Lilith had seen the sense in this, and she'd hugged me fiercely on the morning of our departure. 'You will always have a home here,' she'd said with tears in her eyes. She'd looked at Rodden. 'And you, too.' Finally, she'd glanced at Leap, already sitting atop my brant, and had reached up and given him a pat.

Amis had come forward to bid us goodbye. He'd looked terribly tired, but more at ease than I'd seen him in days. It seemed as if it was finally sinking in that there were to be no more attackers from the north. The sunshine grew stronger every day as the last of the ash cleared from the sky, and the air had lost its preternatural chill. 'We'll build you another turret,' he'd promised Rodden. 'Ten turrets, if you like.' The two friends embraced, and I thought Amis's composure slipped for a moment as they parted. 'I owe you a great deal, old friend,' he murmured.

'And I you,' Rodden had said. 'But don't promise too much, or I'll make you turn the whole palace into turrets.'

It was with a terrifying feeling that I didn't know what came next now that we'd left Pergamia, the twin figures of Amis and Lilith, standing close together in the deserted bailey, shrinking smaller and smaller until they'd disappeared from view.

Now we had arrived in Amentia we were reluctant to land our exhausted brants. The Amentine banner still flew from the ramparts, but how far could you trust a banner? I directed my brant in a low swoop past the castle, as close as I dared go. If Penritha commanded the castle she would associate the enormous birds with me and order her archers to fire. It was one of my brants that had partially blinded her brother.

I spied red and gold uniforms on the battle-ments, the colours of Amentia, not the red and black of Ansengaad. My heart leapt, and unable to hold myself back any longer I flew my brant into the tiny bailey. My mother's soldiers would remember us from the last time we'd landed at the castle and hold their fire.

Several soldiers stood in the bailey and flattened themselves against the wall as we landed, eyes agog. I hailed them, calling, 'Where is the queen?' as my brant lit on the hard packed earth. Rodden's brant thudded to the ground a moment after mine.

It was late afternoon and cold shadows from the high walls fell over us. All was quiet. Overhead, sol-diers peered down at us – my mother's men, but now I saw that there were also a handful dressed in for-eign livery. It was blue and silver. I waved heartily at them, realising they must be the garrisoned men that Amis had sent to aid Renata.

'Well, daughter, what bring you onto our heads now? I have only just flushed out the last lot of troubles you abandoned me with.' Standing across the bailey under an arch stood Renata, poised to show off her queenliness to her best advantage. Her russet curls were arranged just so and her gown was spotless and tasteful. Her words were acerbic but there was amusement on her lips. She looked at Rodden a long moment, sur-prise flashing in her eyes, and then back at me.

I slid from the saddle with as much grace as I could when my legs were stiff from travel. Now that I saw all was well I had leisure to fear what she'd make of seeing Rodden again. I wasn't sure that she'd be glad to find him alive and well. To distract myself I pulled Leap into my arms. He was stiff and cold and I hugged him against my body. Atop the saddle, Griffin shook her feathers out and then let her beak sink wearily back onto her chest.

Travel-grimed and exhausted, Rodden made Renata an excellent leg. 'Your majesty.'

The queen eyed him. 'Rodden Lothskorn. My youngest daughter was pining herself to a shadow over you, nearly inciting a war over you, and you were alive all along.'

I saw Rodden smirk into his sleeve as he rose and I flushed. 'Mother, I did not incite a war over Rodden. If anything it was over Griffin. She –'

'Yes, yes, you must tell me all about it later,' she said, waving us both inside. She accepted my swift kiss with a wrinkle of her nose. 'First, you both need baths. Why do you feel the need to always return home in such a state?'

The fire in Renata's chambers had burned very low by the time we'd got to the end of our evening meal. Rodden and I were in fresh clothes and settled into padded chairs. We hadn't eaten so well in months and I'd stuffed myself full of every favourite childhood delicacy, and a few Pergamian ones Renata had introduced to the kitchens as well. Leap purred steadily on my lap, full of delicacies himself that I'd pilfered from the table for him. Griffin snoozed on the back of my chair, ruffling her feathers every so often as if to prove she wasn't really sleeping, she was simply resting her eyes between bouts of alertness.

'So it was the Pergamian troops that made the difference, your majesty?' Rodden asked, Renata having finished her story of how the siege had ended. She had refused to tell it until she'd heard all of our news, and we'd related all that had happened since I'd fled so mysteriously from the castle. I'd told her about meeting with my father, whom we'd all thought was dead, and she was shocked, but only said, after many minutes' silence, 'He died long ago, poor man.'

'Did you know where he was?' I'd asked.

She'd shaken her head. 'No, I really did think he was dead.' Sadness slackened her features for a moments. 'Perhaps you will tell me about him, one day. I'd like to know.' She reached out and touched my hand. 'But not today. I think it would quite spoil things.'

Now, she sniffed at Rodden's words. 'I wouldn't go so far. No, certainly, we had the upper hand all along. Perhaps the Ansengaad troops were already faltering when the Pergamian soldiers arrived. Yes, the more I think on it the more I think it must have been so.'

Rodden inclined his head deferentially.

'What rot, mother,' I replied. 'I hope you send a particularly grovelling letter of thanks to King Amis as soon as the sun is up tomorrow.'

Renata was indignant. 'I granted him enough favours when I consented to let him marry Lilith. And what a good queen she shall make him.' Her face softened. 'Though I hope it won't be too taxing for her. It is so sudden. But she will do well, I am sure. Now, Lothskorn, I was going to tell you just why we were managing so beautifully before the Pergamian soldiers arrived.'

Rodden shot me an amused look before turning his polite attention to Renata.

'I had been recruiting in secret, you see,' Renata said, 'ever since Zeraphina's enormous birds put the prince's eye out.'

I looked at her in surprise. 'You were?'

'Don't interrupt, daughter. The Amentine capital hasn't held for centuries without some clever work by those that sit atop the throne. We are a small nation, but we protect what is ours. I had my most trusted guards recruiting in the villages and we garrisoned the troops there. I knew things would turn sour with Ansengaad sooner or later. When the inevitable happened and they tried to take the castle I was able to bring all the soldiers out of hiding to defend it.' She looked at Rodden. 'So you see, all was not lost before Amis's assistance. As generous as it was.'

'You had parchments in here, lists and plans,' I recalled. 'You put them away and said they were nothing.'

'Nothing that concerned you, in the state you were in,' she said.

I thought for a moment. 'What did you mean, when the inevitable happened?'

Renata took a sip from her wine glass. 'Daughter, dear, I know you only too well. Marry Prince Folsum? I'd have had an easier time marrying you to the wind.'

'But you tried in any case. When I was … sick,' I said, not knowing how else to refer to my awful dependence on laudanum, 'you insisted I marry him.'

'Only for show. I never thought you'd do it, and I didn't want you to. But it gave me time to try and work out how to get him out of the castle.'

But I'd done that for her. I remembered Folsum's face as I'd shoved him, the look of terror come into his eyes as he realised he wouldn't be able to keep his balance and was going to fall down the stairs. 'I didn't mean to kill him,' I said quietly. 'He was attacking Griffin and it just happened. He was an odious man, but I didn't want him dead. There's been enough death.' I looked at Rodden and knew he was thinking of Servilock. He understood.

A thoughtful silence descended over the table. Renata broke it finally by saying, 'But what of all the harmings? There must be others left, all over Brivora. Lharmell might be destroyed but it could all happen again elsewhere.'

Rodden gave her a look. 'Ah. I have an idea about that.'

'Do you indeed,' she replied, stifling a yawn. 'It can wait till the morning, then. Zeraphina looks like she could curl up right there with her cat and sleep.'

CHAPTER TWENTY-TWO

'What happened to Jaseen?'

Rodden turned away from the window and looked at me. It was a bright, sunny morning and his profile was outlined in gold. A crisp wind blew into the chamber and I pulled my robe tighter about me against the chill. Food to break our fast was spread out on the table in the chamber where we'd eaten the night before, but Renata was nowhere in sight. Likely she'd been up for hours, going about the business of ruling Amentia. Probably Lilith and Amis were doing the same. I, however, had slept and slept until half the morning had gone. Renata had been right; I had been tired. What a luxury it was not to leap from bed before dawn to fight a seemingly endless attacker.

Rodden smiled and asked, 'Jaseen?'

'You know,' I said, yawning and padding to the table to pour a cup of something steaming. 'The vizier's youngest daughter who kept herself alive telling stories so the king wouldn't cut off her head. I didn't hear the end of the story.'

'Oh, there are a thousand stories.'

I joined him at the window and looked up at him critically. 'You need to shave,' I said, rubbing a finger over the stubble. 'Mother will expect you to uphold standards, you know.'

'Ah, but I am her pet just now, did you see? She didn't once try to throw me out or put me in with the pigs. I was given a state room.'

I snorted, most un-princess-like, and said, 'We'll see how long that lasts. But Jaseen, I must know what happened to her.'

He thought a moment. 'Well, after many, many nights of unfinished stories, the king fell in love with her and she with him, and they married and had many sons and daughters.'

'She fell in love him?' I asked, indignant.

He held up his hands, palm out. 'That is the way the story ends. It is just a story.'

I took a mouthful of tea and gazed out the window. There were tiny buds on the swaying trees and an earthy, sappy smell on the breeze. It smelled like coming back to life.

'It's not just a story. I think it might have saved me,' I said.

'Are you going to forgive me again? I liked that,' he murmured into my hair, then kissed it, his arm coming around me and feeling very warm on my shoulder. I remembered his mouth on mine in his turret room, and a hot pang went through me.

There was a cough behind us.

We turned and found Renata standing in the doorway holding a piece of parchment. She looked hard at Rodden's arm until he dropped it. 'I just finished a letter to your sister and the king. I thought you might like to read it.'

I took the letter. The first section told Lilith and Amis that Amentia was safe and Rodden and I, too, and thanked Amis for the troops. The last paragraph made me cry out.

'What is it?' Rodden asked.

I read aloud for his benefit. '"...the bequest of the queendom of Amentia on my eldest daughter, as part of her dowry agreement, I must regretfully withdraw. Recompense for this loss shall be agreed upon at a future date." Mother, why is Lilith not to have Amentia?' Rodden took the letter from me and read it for himself.

'What does Lilith need with it? She is queen of Pergamia.'

'But what will you do with it?'

'I shall rule it,' she said crisply. 'And very well it shall do, too.'

'But you were already going to do that.'

'True. But now, on a day very far into the future, I'm sure, it will be yours.'

I was stunned. Amentia to be mine. It meant I was a young woman of my own means, not destined to be dependent on my sister's kindness or a husband's generosity. It took a long while for this to sink in, but when it did I hugged my mother fiercely, thanking her over and over.

'It will give you a little freedom to make your own decisions,' she said, disentangling herself. 'I'd forgotten how much I enjoyed that privilege as a young woman. You will marry, I suppose, where you will.' She gave Rodden a swift up and down look with pursed lips and took the letter from him. 'But do excuse me. I must send my letter.'

A week later Rodden and I stood by our saddled horses in the bailey. A pack mule was tethered to my saddle and Leap sat on the animal's withers along with our supplies, eyes slitted in the bright sunshine. Griffin flew restlessly from horse to battlements to mule, eager to be off.

Renata stood beneath the arch, placid enough, but with a slight crinkle of disapproval between her eyebrows.

'Do try and be excited for us,' I cajoled her, 'and not think about dull things like propriety.'

'I wasn't thinking about propriety,' she protested. 'I was wondering what I am going to feed your birds.' She glanced at the brants perched atop the bailey walls, free to fly about as they wished.

'They'll catch rats or rabbits. You won't even know they're here.'

'Hmm,' she said, as if she didn't believe me. 'Have you got everything you need?' she asked, noticing

Rodden going through our packs. 'What did you need with that ore from the mines?'

'I didn't tell you my idea, did I, your majesty?' he said, turning. 'When Zeraphina and I were parted in Lharmell and I expected to die in the tunnels, a curious thing happened. None of the harmings died, but all that were Turned became un-Turned. There is something about the yelinate from Amentia that acts as an antidote rather than a poison.'

Rodden had already told me this and I'd grown quite excited by it. I said, 'Now that the tor-line has been destroyed, an un-Turned harming is more or less human, except for the need for blood.'

Renata considered this. 'And you plan to give this antidote to any harmings you find?'

Rodden nodded his assent.

'There must be a great many harmings in the world.'

'Yes, but we hope,' I said, 'that by telling other people about this we won't have to do all the work ourselves. You know now, and your captain of the guard does and has some of this yelbar. We have sent some to King Amis, too.'

'It's a small thing, but it's a start,' she said.

I didn't answer this, but to me it was a very big thing. Not long ago Lharmell was shrouded in almost superstitious mystery. To even speak the words *harming* or *Lharmellin* had been discouraged. And because of that they'd almost won. I was determined that it wasn't going to happen again.

I kissed my mother goodbye and Rodden helped me mount my horse. He bowed to Renata and took his seat astride his own horse.

Now that it had come time to leave some of my excitement dulled, and I felt tears prick my eyes. 'I don't think I like goodbyes,' I said to my mother. 'I think next time I'll sneak away in the night like I usually do. It's easier that way.'

'Nonsense, Zeraphina.' But there was a sheen to her eye as she raised her arm and watched us ride out of the castle gates.

It was a clear, fresh morning with clouds galloping across a blue sky. The road was gravelled and wound steeply down the mountain. Our horses picked their way carefully side by side.

'Where would you like to go first?' Rodden asked.

I thought for a moment. There were so many possibilities. I wanted to drink in every sight at every corner of the land. I wanted to travel across the seas and visit the Jarbin again, the desert people who had helped us. But there was one direction I wanted to go the most, because it was the one that I had feared the most, after the north. Travelling south as an un-Turned harming had always meant the painful tug of the tor-line, and the dreadful fear of something at our backs. But now the tor-line was broken, and we were free to roam where we wished.

'South,' I said, smiling. 'I think I would like to ride south.'

'What a good idea, your highness.'

As the way flattened out we urged our horses into a trot. We rode south, the sun warm on our backs.

THE END